# Killer's Canyon

## WILL C. KNOTT

GEORGE PRIOR
PUBLISHERS
London, England

G.K.HALL&CO.
Boston, Massachusetts
1978

**Library of Congress Cataloging in Publication Data**

Knott, Bill, 1927-
    Killer's Canyon.

    Large print ed.
    1.  Large type books.   I.   Title.
[PZ4.K743Ki 1978]   [PS3561.N645]   813'.5'4   78-16482
ISBN 0-8161-6615-3

Copyright © 1977 by Will C. Knott

Published in Large Print by arrangement with
Doubleday & Company, Inc.

Set in Compugraphic 18 pt English Times

All of the characters in this book are fictitious,
and any resemblance to actual persons, living
or dead, is purely coincidental.

Available for sale in the British Commonwealth
from George Prior Publishers, 37 - 41 Bedford Row,
London, W. C. 1., England

British Commonwealth rights granted courtesy of
Jet Literary Associates, Inc.

ISBN (U. K.)                           0-86043-287-4

# Killer's Canyon

**1**

The distant rattle of rifle fire sounded again. Pulling his black to a halt, Kyle Robinson lifted his head to listen. The ragged sound seemed to have shocked the mountainside around him into a waiting silence. In a moment the echoing roll of gunfire faded, then died away completely. Cursing softly, bitterly, Kyle urged his mount forward again up through the timber, his eyes probing the ridge line above him. Despite his desire to make the ridge as quickly as possible, he refused to punish his big horse into a gallop.

In the time it took him to gain the crest of the ridge, there was no resumption of the gunfire. But it gave him little comfort as he followed the crest to a familiar trail that took him through a thin stand of jack pine on the other side of the ridge.

He rode slack in the saddle to save his

1

mount as he cut down through the timber. He was wearing a short, wool-lined jacket over his shirt and vest, and this high in the Tetons he was glad of its warmth. The wide brim of his flat-crowned Stetson kept his lean face in shadow.

It was a face drawn with fatigue, its high cheekbones prominent, the startlingly blue eyes smoldering under dust-frosted brows. Trouble or the promise of it had caused him to ride hard and far this past week, at times traveling on through moonlit nights. Now that promise had been kept, and the hard reality of this fact was reflected in the grim lines of his face.

Kyle emerged at last onto a small clearing overlooking a lush valley watered by a swift mountain stream. The sun had already dipped below the ridge line behind him, and the valley floor was in shadow. Kyle patted the neck of his mount and peered down intently at the small cluster of ranch buildings that made up the J Bar Ranch.

The ranch sat close beside the stream — an icy, snow-fed torrent Kyle and Jose

Ramirez had fished four years before, after the two men had finished building the log cabin, the lodgepole corrals, the pole-and-shake barn. But the sight of Jose Ramirez's modest spread did not please Kyle. There should have been sleek stock in the lush pastures, horseflesh in the corrals. He should have heard the sound of chickens scolding and scratching from within the barn. In fact, there was no sign of activity. Instead, over the cabin and all the valley there hung an ominous waiting silence.

Suddenly Jose's wife — Kyle recognized the tall, slender woman at once — darted from the cabin and headed for the stream, a wooden bucket in her hand. Alert to her danger by the furtive way she moved, Kyle dismounted swiftly, withdrawing his Winchester from its scabbard. A rifle shot cracked but the woman kept going. The shot had obviously been meant to warn her back, and a small explosion at her feet showed how close the bullet had come. Another shot echoed but the woman continued on to the stream. A third shot caught the bucket in her hand

and sent it flying down the bank and into the stream.

She looked around her then and raised a defiant fist. Then she started back to the cabin. A single shot rang out — from someone obviously infuriated at her courage — and she staggered, then fell. There was a cry from someone near the barn, ordering the rest of the besiegers to hold fire.

No longer firing, those outside the cabin watched the wounded woman try to crawl back to the cabin. At last she ceased crawling and collapsed forward onto the ground. A sense of horror hung over the valley. Kyle felt sick, and then his rage turned him cold as he heard the faint voice of a man crying out in anguish and saw the flash of a revolver coming from the dark rectangle of the cabin doorway. Then Jose darted out of the cabin, grabbed Mary about the shoulders and tried to pull her into the cabin. This brought a quick resumption of the firing, and Kyle saw one bullet slam Jose back against the cabin wall. Still holding on to Mary, however, Jose pulled her back inside.

The firing was a steady fusillade now as Kyle swiftly, silently descended the steep slope, his eyes searching the bushes and rocks below him as the darkness fell swiftly over the valley.

\* \* \*

It was entirely dark now and the moon had yet to rise, and Pete Bushnell was resigned to another night of this miserable business. On Sheriff Allison's orders he had moved closer to the greaser's cabin to make sure the man didn't make a break for it during the night.

This had been Rick's job the night before and he guessed it was only fair that tonight should be his turn. He was now crouched behind the corral fence with a clear view of the cabin doorway. For the last fifteen minutes or so, not a shot had been fired at the cabin, and Ramirez had kept himself away from the still open doorway.

It was an ugly business, but this man was a murderer as well as a goddamned rustler. He deserved what he was getting. Then Pete thought of Ramirez's wife. It was not pleasant to think he had been a party to that. Something about it had grabbed him, and he had flung his rifle up to his shoulder and started to squeeze off shot after shot. But it was not his bullet that had hit her. It had come from south of the cabin, probably Rick or Frenchie — trying to cut it just a little too fine.

Pete shuddered in spite of himself and felt an increasing resentment for Ramirez. It was his fault. If he hadn't killed Beecher's son . . .

The sound of someone splashing across the stream came to him. He turned to see who it was, but at that distance he could not make out the face. He was rangy and moved quick, like Johnny Lomax, the sheriff's deputy. But Pete couldn't be sure in the darkness.

Pete didn't know any of these hardcases too well. He had just gone along because Carol had told him it was his duty to back Mr. Beecher. Pete shook his head at the thought. That Carol. She was thinking all the time. Beecher was the biggest man in these parts and not only owned the hardware store where Pete worked, but the bank, the mill and most of the best grazing land in the Wind River Basin. Yep, Beecher would sure remember Pete for this, him going after the man who had rustled his cattle and then bushwhacked his son.

"That you, Johnny?"

The man pulled up beside Pete and nodded.

Pete took a deep breath and looked back at the cabin, glad of the company. It was so dark he could no longer make out the cabin doorway.

"Where's the horses?" Pete's companion asked softly, as he settled down beside him.

"Didn't the sheriff tell Frenchie and Rick to take care of them tonight?" Pete replied, mildly surprised at the question. "They're grazing by the cottonwoods in the flat." He glanced at Lomax. The man's hat brim almost completely hid his face. "You thinking of pulling out?"

"It's a thought," Lomax replied.

Pete found himself thinking of Carol

again. He had been a long time without his wife. Too long. Too damn long. "What about Ramirez?"

Lomax shrugged.

Pete looked back at the cabin and considered the situation. With every passing second the thought of leaving this high country and cutting out for home filled him with delicious anticipation. It was a damn good idea, at that. If Ramirez wasn't dead, he sure as hell was close to it. They'd done enough for Beecher, for Christ's sake. Three days up here was enough — more than enough.

"I think we should pull out," Pete said abruptly. "What's the sheriff think?"

The deputy shrugged.

"You think we done enough, Johnny?" Pete asked hopefully. "If you do, I'll go tell him what you said. I'd sure as hell like to cut out. That business with the greaser's woman was a real turkey shoot. We won't get any more chances like that. Ramirez won't let us."

"That was a turkey shoot, all right," Lomax said, his voice strangely cold. "You liked that, huh?"

Hell no, Pete thought. He hadn't *liked* it. You'd have to be an Indian to like that sort of thing. But he wanted to impress the sheriff's deputy, so he shrugged. "Sure. Why not? She was just a greaser, like her old man."

Lomax nodded and turned to face Pete. "Go see the sheriff," he said, his voice soft now, sibilant.

Something in his voice warned Pete — sent a shiver of apprehension down his back. Looking closely now at the man's dark, impassive face, he felt a sudden paralyzing fear. *This man was not Johnny Lomax!*

"Sure. Sure, Johnny," Pete managed, pulling away. "I'll go see the sheriff. I'll go right now."

Pete snatched up his rifle and pushed himself back until he reached the stream bank. Crouching low, he started upstream on his way to the barn where he knew the sheriff was. When he looked back toward the cabin, he was just able to make out the dim figure still crouched by the corral fence. Who the hell was he? And why was he dealing himself in like this?

And then it occurred to him: *He's a friend of the greaser!*

The thought stopped him in his tracks. A sudden, reckless bravado caused him to swing his rifle around . . .

\* \* \*

Kyle had been watching the young fellow move off. Kyle knew the fellow had discovered he was not a part of the posse. He hoped now that the kid wouldn't make any dumb moves.

Then he saw the dark shadow outlined against the stream stop and turn suddenly and caught the glint of the young man's rifle barrel. Throwing himself flat, he sighted and fired, all in one swift motion. The fellow uttered a soft cry and disappeared behind the bank. A moment later Kyle heard something strike the water — just as the rest of the posse, startled into action by the shot, resumed firing at the cabin.

Still flat on the ground, Kyle waited for the fusillade to ease up, noting as he did just where the flashes of gunfire were coming from — and the number of them. There were four posse members still out there at least. One was behind the barn. Since that kid had been heading in that direction, Kyle assumed that this was where the sheriff was holed up. Another one was firing from the cottonwoods north of the cabin. Two others were firing from downstream, and these were obviously the men that young fool had said were taking care of the posse's horses.

Kyle waited patiently as the lead whined overhead and thunked into the cabin's side. In the darkness the posse was obviously unaware of what had happened and could only have assumed that either the kid guarding the cabin door or Jose had fired the shot.

Gradually, with no return fire from the cabin, the posse's enthusiasm for throwing good lead after bad gave up. They ceased firing and Kyle started to crawl across the open ground toward the cabin. He kept his head low and did not hurry. Any noise he made would be caught by Jose, assuming the man was still alive.

Less than a yard from the open doorway, Kyle called Jose's name softly. There was no answer. Kyle called a second time, louder.

This time Jose answered. His voice sounded dim and scratchy. "Kyle! You crazy sonofabitch! Get in here!"

Kyle took a deep breath at the sound of Jose's voice and pulled himself the rest of the way into the cabin. At once his left hand came down on Mary's dress. He caught her arm then. It was cold. He pulled his hand away.

"Over here," Jose called softly. "In this corner, Kyle."

The interior of the cabin was as black as pitch, and the corner to which Jose directed Kyle was to his right. When he reached his friend's side, he saw that Jose had poked a hole in the chinking between the logs, enabling him to see out across the yard as far as the mountainside beyond. The blackness of the cabin's interior seemed to give an uncanny illumination to the world outside.

Jose reached out and took Kyle's hand. "Mary is dead, *amigo,*" Jose said. "She

12

is there by the door. They gave her a chance to get out earlier, but she would not go from me." He shook his head in anguish. "I pleaded with her. Then I got hit and mentioned how thirsty I was and she went out for water. She only said, 'You thirsty. Get water . . .' Sonofabitch! I should never have told her."

Jose was sitting with his back to the wall, and in the darkness Kyle could not be sure how badly he had been hit. But Jose did not sound good. "How bad are you hit?" Kyle asked.

"It is all right, Kyle. I sit still and do not bleed much."

"Where you hit?"

"The first time in the left arm. The second time, when I went after Mary, in the chest. The arm, she is broken. That other feels like one big branding iron sitting on my chest. That is the big one, I think, *amigo*."

As Kyle's eyes adjusted to the darkness, he gained a clearer picture of his friend. Jose's dark, lean face was gaunt, his eyes like dark wounds. The man was obviously in great pain.

"I got your telegram late, Jose," Kyle explained. "But I came as soon as I got it."

"You came, *amigo*. That is enough."

"What is all this? Your telegram said you were accused of murder and might go to jail. Did you break out?"

"No, Kyle. I got a good lawyer, and the judge, he is an honest man. And this big rancher, Beecher, he had no proof I kill his son. They just find him dead on my land. I am innocent, Kyle. I do not kill any man."

"So what's a posse doing out there?"

"Beecher. He owns the sheriff. Someone hang a steer in my barn. Beecher's men find it, so now they come after me for rustling. One way or another, they think they get me for killing Beecher's son. And this time no lawyer, no judge. I will dance at the end of a rope first. But they will have to come in here and get me."

Kyle shook his head. "I should have got here sooner."

"Do not trouble yourself, *amigo*. Like I say, you came and that is enough. Now it is like old times, hey? You and me against the townies."

Kyle wished he could share his friend's enthusiasm. He glanced over at the dim outline of Mary's body and shook his head. Never in his life would he forget that scene — and Jose trying to drag his dead wife into the safety of this battered cabin.

He looked back at Jose. "The posse left a man — a young kid, really — out there by the corral to watch the cabin door," Kyle explained. "He's not there now, Jose. And before this posse finds that out, I think we better see if we can get out of here — maybe make it to the stream and let it carry us down to the flats below the cabin. I think that's where they're keeping their horses."

"Sure, Kyle."

At once Jose stirred himself and began to push himself erect. As he did so he uttered a groan that seemed to have been wrung from the very roots of his soul. Reaching out quickly, Kyle helped him to his feet. Jose grabbed the windowsill with his good arm and managed a bleak grin.

"Don't touch the right arm, *amigo,*"

Jose warned. "When I try to pull Mary inside, I make it some worse, I think."

When they reached the door, Jose paused and looked back at Mary's crumpled body.

"We should not leave her like this," he said.

"I'll come back for her, Jose," Kyle said. "I promise."

Kyle's promise was enough for Jose. He ducked before Kyle out into the moonless night. Kyle followed and they kept low and reached the stream undetected. Kyle had to help Jose down the embankment. When Jose waded into the icy waters, he gasped but kept going until the stream closed about his waist. Then he dipped his head and drank his fill.

Afterward, he straightened and started downstream, holding onto his broken arm. Kyle stayed right beside him, should he stumble and fall. Kyle had hung his gunbelt around his neck and was holding his Winchester well out of the water.

They had not gone more than twenty yards when Kyle caught sight of the young man he had shot in front of the cabin.

The stream had carried his body into a shallow pool near the bank. The swift water was tugging at his legs and in a moment he would be swept back out into the stream.

Kyle slogged over and, grabbing the man by the back of his vest, dragged him up onto the embankment well out of the water. He leaned close in order to catch a heartbeat if there was one. There was, faint but steady. Then Kyle inspected the man's wound. The bullet had entered high on the left shoulder, shattering the shoulder bone. In the poor light Kyle could not tell if the bullet had gone on through.

The young man's eyes flickered once, then opened. At sight of Kyle bending over him, he started to raise himself and cry out. Kyle brought his right fist around in a hard, sledging blow that caught the man flush on his chin. The jawbone cracked and Kyle saw the fellow's eyes snap shut again. He stuffed the man's bandanna into the shoulder wound in an effort to staunch the flow of blood, then waded back into the water after Jose.

He caught up with him just as they approached a sharp bend in the stream. Beyond this point the stream entered the flat. But the way was not clear. On a small bluff overlooking the stream, the two members of the posse who were guarding the horses had built a fire and were sitting around it, their rifles propped beside them.

Kyle tugged at Jose's shirt and indicated the embankment under the bluff. Jose nodded and waded in under the bluff where the stream had cut well into it before sluicing away into the flat. Both of them were glad to get out of the icy water and find dry ground. Jose slumped down and closed his eyes almost at once. Kyle knelt on one knee beside him.

"I'm going up there to see to those two," Kyle whispered to Jose. "Can you sit a horse?"

Jose nodded without opening his eyes.

There was still no moon, but Kyle was able to make out his friend's face clearly. It did not look good. The cold water had chilled him brutally. His complexion was almost blue and his teeth were chattering uncontrollably.

Kyle glanced up at the face of the embankment. He decided he would have to go around, come at the two from the direction of the flat. Both of them were sitting on the same side of the fire, facing the cabin upstream. Kyle followed the stream's channel into the flat, then slogged ashore and dropped to the ground.

The grass was tall and lush all the way to the crest of the bluff. Kyle began to move through it with the stealth and patience of a large mountain cat after a long winter.

\* \* \*

Frenchie Wells and Rick Warner were both unhappy at the prospect of spending another long night in the chill high country. But at least they had a fire.

Frenchie, heavier and taller than Rick, was the darker and older of the two. During the last six years they had been through a lot together and had both ridden north with Clay Allison, the newly appointed sheriff of Cody. Now, chewing on a long stem of grass, Frenchie considered the ill-starred course this vendetta of Beecher's had followed.

They had missed an opportunity to bushwhack the greaser outside of Cody. Then, after following him up here, Allison had let that greenhorn kid, Pete Bushnell, open fire too soon, enabling the greaser to make it back into the cabin safely. He was still in there now — and still trouble.

Frenchie had a gut-deep anxiety about this whole business. He wanted to get rid of the greaser soon — and clear out of this place. They had caught the greaser for sure that last time — and his woman. But it sure as hell hadn't been pretty. Rick had admitted that it had been his shot that hit her. He had tried to scare her with a bullet past her left cheek. Frenchie shook his head at the thought. Sometimes he wondered about Rick.

Frenchie shifted restlessly on the log, reached over for the stick he was using and poked the fire back to life. Winter came fast in this high country and he could feel its chill on his neck already.

"You thinking what I'm thinking?" Rick asked.

Frenchie turned to face him. "It's getting pretty damn cold up here and this operation is turning into work. Right?"

Rick grinned crookedly at his partner. His long, shaggy blond hair hung down over one side of his face, giving him a mongrelly look that added some to the menace he inspired in others. "You said it, Frenchie. You damn well put your finger on the problem. Me for the warmer spots. I think I'd rather burn to death than freeze to death."

Frenchie looked back at the fire. He usually did know pretty well what Rick was thinking — sometimes even before Rick knew himself.

"Give it one more day, Rick," he said. "Then maybe we'll quit this high country for good."

"That's about my limit, too. But what about Clay?"

"He's the sheriff now, all legal and proper. So I reckon he just might stay on here and keep milkin' this big rancher."

"He won't milk Beecher if he don't

get this greaser's scalp for him."

Frenchie nodded. "That's so."

"Which means sooner or later one of us is going to have to go in there after that Mex."

"Not us," said Frenchie, his dark face growing darker with resolve. "Not us. Lomax or that kid, Bushnell."

"Yeah. I'm betting on Bushnell. He's so all-fired eager to impress his boss." Rick chuckled. "Leastways, we got the greaser's squaw."

"You mean *you* did. And that's small comfort. Beecher wants the greaser — not his woman."

Frenchie pulled his poncho closer about his lean sholders and found himself thinking of the long trail up from Texas. And the sleepy cowtowns along the way. Most of them were already full up with sod busters and their nits. And the women in their bonnets and cold stares. The country was getting too damned civilized. They'd had to cut through more and more barbed wire after Abilene. Barbed wire. Frenchie shook his head at the thought. And the telegraph. That really turned him grizzly. Like Clay said, the damned telegraph made it near impossible to get clean away from a raise. But not quite. Frenchie smiled at the thought of the Bordentown raise last spring. They'd cut the wires before riding in and got clean away as a result.

But there weren't going to be any more jobs like that. It was no longer easy getting the men, for one thing. Frenchie picked up his stick to resume poking at the fire. That was when he heard Rick sigh, the way a horse does when a heavy saddle is lifted off after a long ride. As Frenchie turned, he saw Rick settle loosely forward onto the fire.

Still turning, Frenchie saw the arm coming down, the gun barrel gleaming in the light from the fire. He tried to raise his right arm to ward off the blow. But all he could manage was to deflect it a little. The barrel slammed down through the crown of his hat and caught him on the side of the head. The blow staggered him but he managed to pull away, stepping close to the fire as he did so.

It was no use. He couldn't raise his

23

arms. Out of the night someone tall and rangy advanced on him, brought his six-gun around with punishing force and caught Frenchie on the side of his face.

Frenchie lost consciousness before he hit the ground.

\* \* \*

Kyle holstered his Colt and pulled the lanky, blond fellow out of the fire. The gunman's shirt was smoldering and the flesh on his neck had begun to pucker. Kyle used the man's rifle to prop him back up on the log. Next he dragged the fellow's companion over and hunched him up on the log alongside his friend. Then Kyle threw a few more sticks on the fire and moved quickly back down the bluff to the stream.

He found Jose still on his back. For a moment he was afraid the man was unconscious. But as soon as Kyle reached his side, Jose opened both eyes and looked up at him.

"What took you, *amigo?* There were only two of them."

Kyle reached down and helped Jose to his feet. The man compressed his lips to keep from crying out when Kyle inadvertently touched his broken arm. Kyle fashioned a sling for it with his bandanna, then helped Jose to splash through the bed of the stream and out onto the flat.

The horses were bunched in the shadow of a cottonwood grove close to the stream. Kyle could make out the dim huddle of saddles in a heap under one of the trees. He let Jose down so that he could rest with his back to one of the trees and then, working swiftly in the darkness, he took the hobbles off each of the horses and then saddled two of them. He helped Jose onto one of the animals and handed the reins up to Jose's good left hand.

"My black is on the trail above the valley," he told Jose. "Can you find the trail?"

"I can find it."

"I'll give you a start before I scatter the horses."

Jose nodded, clapped his heels feebly to the flanks of his mount and started across the flat toward the trail. Kyle watched until Jose disappeared into the night. Then he mounted the horse he had selected, rode over to the rest of the horses and herded them away from the cottonwoods. Then he took out his six-gun and fired into the air. The horses bolted away from him in a single mass. He clapped spurs to his mount and took after them, firing as he went. Necks stretching, they surged into a full gallop and in a moment were out of sight in the darkness. He pulled up and listened.

Behind him he heard faint shouts. Ahead of him he heard the rapidly dying thunder of the stampeding animals. Kyle knew this valley well. There would be no barrier to their headlong flight for at least a couple of miles, and if they found the Peace River Pass, they'd be in Sweetwater country in the morning.

The shouting behind him was getting louder. Kyle turned his horse and galloped through the darkness after Jose.

## 2

The moment Carl Beecher saw the four men ride wearily through the Double B gate, he knew there was trouble and left the porch to meet them.

Joanne had seen them enter also. She hurried from the stable and joined her father as the four men pulled up and dismounted in front of the cookshack.

It was Joanne who spoke first, her voice iced with contempt: "You botched it. The Mex got away."

Clay Allison thumbed his hat back, revealing his thick shock of white hair, and squared his shoulders. He was as tall as Beecher, heavily built and still powerful. At the moment his dark eyes blazed out fiercely at the girl. But she was right; his news was bad and that gave her the edge. Allison looked away from her and turned to face Beecher.

"The Mex had a friend, looks like," the sheriff told Beecher. "We don't know where he came from, but he hit us while we was bottlin' up the Mex in his cabin. He shot up Pete Bushnell, busted his jaw and stampeded the horses on us."

Beecher looked from Allison to Frenchie Wells and his sidekick, Rick Warner. The two men looked awful. "This friend of Ramirez have anything to do with the condition of Frenchie and Rick here?" he asked Allison.

The sheriff nodded grimly. "They were both unconscious when Johnny and I found them. And they were no help at all in rounding up the horses."

Beecher felt some pity for both men. A mean gash had laid open Frenchie's right cheekbone, and that side of his face had swollen to the size and consistency of an overripe plum. The man's right eye was completely hidden behind a thick fold of shiny, discolored flesh.

Rick Warner's eyes were red-rimmed and bleary. He seemed to be having continuous difficulty focusing. It was obvious he had been struck a fearful blow on the head.

Beecher had once seen a similar look on the face of a blacksmith who had been kicked by a mule. The man had never regained his former efficiency.

"Who was this fellow?" Beecher asked Allison.

"Damned if I know. That Mex didn't have no friends around here."

"Well, what did he look like?" Joanne demanded. "You can at least give us a description of him, can't you?"

"No, we can't," Allison told her shortly. He looked back at Beecher. "Frenchie and Rick, they were hit so sudden, they never got a clean look at him. And Pete Bushnell, he's got a shot-up collarbone and a busted jaw. He ain't been able to do nothing but groan. We had to leave him back there."

"And what about Ramirez?"

"He and that friend of his got clean away, looks like," Allison admitted. "But we wounded him at least once. I saw him get hit."

Johnny Lomax spoke up then, anxious to take some heat off Allison. "We got the greaser's woman."

"You what?" demanded Beecher.

"I mean we killed the greaser's wife," Lomax said.

Beecher took a deep breath.

"I see," said Joanne nastily. "You men were not able to bring in the man who murdered my brother, but you *were* able to shoot down his wife. And after that accomplishment, you let some stranger you didn't even see, apparently, tear you all to pieces, spook your horses and then get clean away with Ramirez."

Johnny Lomax's mouth became a hard line as he listened to Joanne, and Beecher saw sullen hatred appear on the faces of the men. His daughter was riding them too hard.

"Back off, Joanne," he told her. "These men don't need your tongue."

"Back off!" she cried, swinging around to face him. "Back off! You mean go easy on these fools! And you sent all the way to Texas for such men"

She spun and strode furiously back toward the house. Before she reached it, she began to run and Beecher realized she was crying. Not in sorrow, but in fury and frustration.

Beecher looked back at the four men. Despite their bedraggled appearance, they were still a formidable group dedicated to implementing his will and he was not ready yet to write them off. Not after what he had had to do to get Allison that sheriff's badge.

"How soon can you and your men go after Ramirez?" Beecher asked Allison.

Allison replied quickly. "Give us fresh mounts and some grub and we'll be out of here in less'n an hour."

"Well, you know what I want, Clay. As the sheriff of this county, you had every right to bring in Ramirez. Now that he has resisted, you have no choice but to go after him and bring him in — dead or alive. And you know which way I prefer it."

Beecher spoke this last grimly and forcefully — but unhappily. It was not that he disagreed with what he had to do. He just did not like having to put it as bluntly as that in front of these men.

"We'll get him this time, Mr. Beecher," Lomax said.

"See that you do."

"We should take care of that Bushnell kid first," Allison said.

Beecher frowned. Of course. Damn it! He had almost forgotten about Bushnell. "What will you need?"

"A flatbed wagon to get him into town, so's the doc can take a look at him. Johnny can take him."

"No. I'll send Joanne with you. She can take Bushnell back to Cody. I'll want her to calm down Pete's wife, anyhow. And this way you and Lomax won't have to split up. I want you to keep after those two until you get them." He frowned suddenly. "Did you bury the greaser's wife?"

"No."

"I see. You just left her there for the buzzards and the coyotes."

"Hell, she was just an Indian."

"Leaving her there like that won't set well, Clay. I suggest you take the time to bury her."

The man nodded. "We'll see to it."

"Now go find cookie. Fill your bellies and get what provisions you need. Joanne will be able to move out in less than an hour."

Beecher watched them move off. Until now he had had great confidence in Clay Allison. Clay was a hard, relentless man. But leaving that dead woman as an advertisement — that *was* botching it, just as Joanne had said.

He turned wearily and followed after his daughter, his concern suddenly focused on her. Joanne's grief at the death of her brother had equaled, perhaps even surpassed, his own. That grief, and her obsession with getting Ramirez, seemed to have driven every humane impulse out of her, making her almost impossible to handle. It troubled him deeply to see her like this. He had already lost a son, and now it almost seemed he was in danger of losing his daughter as well. Unless Ramirez was brought in soon — and this time without any Boston lawyer or mealymouthed judge to get him off — his daughter just might go after Ramirez herself.

But he understood Joanne's rage perfectly. It was she — alone — who had first come upon her brother's body.

The way Marshal Borrmann had

described it to him, Joanne had ridden on ahead as usual and come upon Jed's body lying face down in Ramirez's north pasture. The back of Jed's head had been blown out, his six-gun still in his holster. Joanne had been almost out of her mind as she galloped back across the flat to tell Borrmann and the others.

But if it was not surprising why she wanted the death of Ramirez, his own reason for wanting the same thing was just as powerful as hers. If she had lost a brother, he had lost a son.

Beecher paused for a moment as his sense of loss swept over him again — that searing ache he felt whenever he allowed himself to truly consider it. He reached out a powerful, gnarled hand and took hold of the porch post. Well into his sixties, Beecher's thick head of hair was snow-white, his drooping mustache as gray as alkali dust. But he was still a tall, powerfully built man with square shoulders and coal-black eyes that peered out now with uncommon vigor from under beetling brows. And yet, something essential had gone out of him with the death of his son.

Others noted it and he felt it. For he too had shared his daughter's pride in Jed. So many times he had found himself wishing his wife could have lived long enough to see how straight her firstborn had grown. And always the sight of Jed riding toward him — tall in the saddle, frank and yet easygoing, with a gentleness he had inherited from his mother — had warmed him like sunlight on a weathered cliff . . .

Abruptly, Beecher shook himself free of these reflections, straightened his tall frame and strode on into the big house, continuing on down the main hall to Jed's room. He knew he would find Joanne in there, sitting in Jed's big wing chair by the window.

He was not wrong.

\*     \*     \*

Kyle snatched up his Winchester and moved swiftly, silently to the door of the line shack and peered out. He could see nothing through the pines. And he was not sure if that *was* a horse he had heard.

Then he saw the big buck step out of the trees, antlered head high, nose testing the wind. Kyle relaxed and leaned his rifle against the wall and went back to Jose.

The stump of a candle was guttering on the shelf over Jose's bunk. In its dim light Kyle saw Jose turn his head toward him. The wounded man's lips moved, but Kyle could hear nothing.

He leaned closer.

"Mary . . ." Jose whispered through cracked lips. "Don't leave her . . ."

Kyle patted the man's shoulder and when Jose tried to raise his arm to pull Kyle still closer, Kyle restrained him. "Take it easy now," he said gently. "No hurry about that. Can't leave you like this."

The man's eyes became suddenly bright and for a brief moment seemed to pierce Kyle's soul. "Yes . . . can leave me . . . soon."

Kyle was about to argue with the man, but he did not have the heart for it. He placed his hand gently on Jose's forehead. Jose was burning up. The dying man spoke the truth. He was already in hell and knew it.

Kyle shook his head in bitter frustration. It had been a long ride he had made only to find at the end of it that he must bury the one person he cared for most in this world. The desolate ache he had been living with this past night became an almost intolerable anguish.

Kyle and Jose had been kids when they first met, growing up on the same huge ranch in Oklahoma. And though one was Mexican and the other of doubtful parentage, there were none on that spread to call either of them for it — or make them feel ashamed. They had become closer than brothers . . .

Jose stirred and groaned suddenly, pulling Kyle back to the present. Kyle reached for his canteen, unstoppered it, and placed its tip into Jose's mouth. The man drank in short, convulsive gulps. When he began to cough, Kyle pulled the canteen away. Jose managed a smile.

"That was good, *amigo*. After all these years, you are still my blood brother, eh?" He reached out a bony hand and caught Kyle's wrist and pulled him closer with surprising strength. "You will see to those butchers . . ."

"Yes, Jose," Kyle replied quietly. "I will see to them. I will see to all of them."

Jose released Kyle and sank back, nodding his head and closing his eyes. He seemed to breathe easier. "That is good, my friend," he murmured softly.

He grew quiet. Kyle again placed his open palm on Jose's forehead. The man was still burning up. A quick inspection of the chest wound told Kyle why. The wound had gone black around the edges. He could smell it. And there was nothing Kyle could do.

After a moment of contemplating Jose's still features, Kyle got wearily to his feet and went back to the line shack's doorway and looked out at the cold, sunlit morning. A lark's bright call echoed in the meadow below the pines, its flight song an unsettling contrast to the grim business behind him. The clean sparkle of the mountain morning seemed only to increase Kyle's sense of loss.

The day had been this bright, Kyle remembered, when Jose and he had found themselves alone in town one afternoon while the rancher went about his business. The townies had gathered at once, forming a circle around them, like coyotes around a couple of rabbits. Kyle was the bastard, Jose the Mex. First came the names, then the taunts, and finally the combined assault.

There had been six townies all told, but when the dust settled Jose and Kyle were still on their feet, their faces swollen but their knuckles bloody. That was when they shook hands and became what they had been ever since — blood brothers.

As he looked back on it, Kyle smiled briefly. That had been a good time and there had been others just as good, all during the years they were growing into manhood. The rancher, Colonel Mordecai Robinson, had seen to it that all the children of the men and women who worked on his huge spread were made to go to the school he himself had established for that purpose. The school's schedule was never allowed to conflict with that of spring roundup, of course, so that when Kyle and Jose were ready to strike out on their own, they found that they not only could read and write, but they could find a job on any ranch as well, and be rated top hands. It had been a good life, growing up on that spread. Kyle couldn't imagine any better way to bring up a boy. And someday, perhaps . . .

But there was no sense in thinking of that now. Jose's attempt to build his own spread, modest though it was, had been doomed from the start. This time the townies had won.

Kyle heard Jose groan softly and call his name. He turned swiftly and hurried back into the shack.

At midmorning of that same day, Kyle placed his hat back on his head and walked slowly away from the freshly turned earth that covered Jose Ramirez. Kyle had selected what he felt was a suitable spot — a grassy ledge that overlooked a long, gentle sweep of meadowland. The grassland extended to the forested slopes of two snow-capped peaks that shouldered magnificently into the high clean air. With such headstones, Kyle felt, Jose and Mary would sleep well.

As Kyle rode off a few minutes later to

bring Mary back to the spot he had prepared for her beside Jose, he thought again of that promise he had made to Jose — to find and punish those butchers. And when he remembered that promise, he felt a welcome, reckless rage. He could taste it, feel it take control of him.

It was almost enough rage to mask the deep hammering grief he felt.

Kyle could see Mary's body just inside the doorway. It was late in the afternoon of that same day, and as Kyle glanced skyward he saw a single buzzard coasting high overhead. He dismounted and moved quickly into the cabin and past Mary's body, looking for a sheet and some blankets.

He was pulling them off the bed when the cabin doorway behind him darkened. Kyle spun to see the young man from the posse he had shot and then saved from drowning. But that had been a fool weak thing to have done and Kyle was sorry for it now — abysmally sorry.

The kid had his six-gun in his hand and was leaning shakily on the doorjamb while he glared murderously at Kyle through pain-glazed eyes. He was as silent as death standing there and Kyle realized he must have broken the fellow's jaw when he knocked him out.

The two stared at each other for a long moment. Then shakily, but with grim purpose and an iron resolve, the kid raised the six-gun he was holding and sighted along its barrel. Kyle did not wait a second longer. He threw himself to one side and drew his own gun, clearing leather so swiftly that even as the gun in the kid's hand roared, Kyle's gun was coming up. The bullet slammed into the wall by the bed and the kid took a wooden step into the cabin and fired straight ahead a second time. And a third time.

Kyle crouched to one side. He held his fire and watched as the injured man continued blindly toward the bed, still pulling off shot after shot. Just as he reached the bed, the hammer of his six-gun came down on an empty chamber and the man stumbled forward and collapsed upon the mattress.

Kyle holstered his weapon and stepped quickly to the unconscious man's side and turned him over. The fellow's eyes were open wide. But he did not see Kyle and would see nothing living again.

A quick examination showed Kyle why. The bullet that shattered his shoulder had not gone on through. It had angled down into his chest, most likely lodging in his lungs. Kyle rolled the young man back over onto his face, snatched the sheets and blanket up off the floor where he had dropped them and hurried over to Mary's body.

Kyle had just draped his burden over the pommel and swung into the saddle when he heard the soft thunder of horses' hooves crossing the flat below the cabin. The kid's gunshots were bringing whoever it was at a gallop. As he roweled his black into the stand of cottonwoods north of the cabin, Kyle realized at once who these riders must be. Double B's Texas gunslingers coming back after their wounded man.

Once safely into the cottonwoods, Kyle flung himself from his horse, tied up his black and snatched his Winchester from its scabbard along with a couple of boxes of shells from a saddlebag. He moved swiftly back until he could see the cabin through the trees. Moving more cautiously after that, he found a cottonwood at the edge, broke open the boxes of shells and levered a cartridge into the Winchester's firing chamber.

Then he waited.

He did not have long to wait. Four riders and a woman driving a flatbed wagon pounded up to the cabin. The riders dismounted and one of them, obviously the leader, strode into the cabin to return almost at once with the news of what he found. Kyle watched closely.

Then, as he had expected, one of the men found Kyle's tracks. At once the four men remounted and started to follow them towards the cottonwoods. Kyle could not be sure, but he was almost certain he could hear the woman's shrill voice urging them on.

Kyle fitted the rifle to his cheek, sighted

carefully and fired. The foremost rider spun off his horse and disappeared into the thick, tufted grass. Kyle pumped and fired a second time, putting the remaining riders into frantic flight back toward the cabin.

The woman seemed furious at their good sense and began urging them to go back. Kyle aimed carefully at a spot just in front of her team of horses and fired. Even at that distance he could see the spurt of dust that kicked up at the horses' feet. With a shrill whinny the frightened animals reared. Kyle fired again. This time the woman leaped from the wagon and joined the others in a flight to the cabin.

Kyle put two quick shots through the still open doorway and then bellied down beside the tree. There was no sign of movement from the man he had dropped with his first shot. He dismissed him, put his sights on the already shattered window over the kitchen, pulled off just a little bit, then fired. He heard the smack of the slug in the logs, waited a moment for the warning to sink in, then put two quick shots through the window. He moved his sights and put another shot through the doorway, levered a fresh cartridge into the firing chamber, and waited.

He could hear the murmur of unhappy voices coming from the cabin. Abruptly there was a shot, followed by the thunk of a bullet as it lodged in the tree above him. Kyle moved further back behind the trunk and then put two more shots through the window. Loud, bitter cursing followed this exchange, and then silence.

Kyle relaxed, reached into his vest pocket and pulled out his Bull Durham and built himself a cigarette. It was getting chilly and soon it would be dark. Already a cold upland mist was moving along the surface of the stream and across the flats below the cabin.

A head appeared in the window. Kyle sighted swiftly and squeezed off a shot. A chip of wood from the window frame just above the man's head flew into the air. Before Kyle could fire again, the head ducked back out of sight. When no further heads appeared at the window, Kyle realized they had gotten his message.

He was still out here and still watching.

Dusk came on swiftly after that. As it deepened, Kyle put occasional shots into the cabin just to impress upon its occupants his accuracy and his persistence — and to give them a small taste of what it must have been like for Jose and his wife.

At last, as darkness settled finally over the valley, Kyle sent four quick shots at the cabin, waited for a moment or two, then rose and faded back into the cottonwoods. Reaching his black, he untied it and vaulted into the saddle, guiding the animal as swiftly as the fading light would allow through the timber.

He was not worried about finding his way back to the line shack, nor was he worried about these men being able to follow his trail in the dark. They would not be able to track him until morning. And when they reached the place where he had buried Jose and Mary sometime tomorrow, Kyle would be well on his way into Cody.

He needed to know more than the dying Jose had been able to tell him. This meant he would have to seek out the lawyer who had defended Jose. And perhaps also the judge who had dismissed the murder charge against Jose for lack of evidence. The lawyer's name was Landon. Kyle had not been able to catch the name of the judge. But both men — according to Jose — had shown great courage in standing up to the Double B and freeing Jose despite Beecher's threats.

First, then, Kyle would find the lawyer and see what he knew. Then, when Kyle was ready, he would see to those men behind him in the darkness — see to them as finally and as ruthlessly as they had seen to Jose and Mary.

# 3

As Joanne Beecher turned the flatbed wagon onto Front Street, she kept her dark eyes straight ahead and did her best to ignore those following her progress from the board walks and the barefoot urchins racing ahead of her with the news.

The bright white silk of her blouse was in startling contrast to her black, wide-brimmed hat and split skirt. She was a beautiful woman with long chestnut hair and strong, rather than pretty, features. But at the moment she presented a grim and formidable appearance to all those who watched her pass.

A few horsemen riding in the opposite direction turned their horses as she passed so they could gain a better view of the two blanketed corpses in the back of the wagon. The blanket had worked itself off Bushnell's boots during the long, jolting ride from the greaser's cabin, but she had been too weary to stop the team and get off to adjust it. No one as yet knew whose bodies she was carrying into town, but she could understand the speculation that now raced ahead of her down Front Street. Just before she turned the corner she had overheard one lathered cowboy bellow into a saloon that Joanne Beecher had killed the greaser and was bringing in his body.

She drove her team straight down Front Street until she came to the barber shop, where she pulled up. By that time a sizable crowd had gathered. Three of the young boys who had been racing after her down the street, in an effort to get a peek at the bodies, were quickly chased away — to make more room for the adults.

Looking to her side for the first time since entering Cody, she saw the crowd — hushed and expectant — and Burnside standing in front of his barber shop. Burnside was watching her intently, a foam-flecked straight razor in his right hand. She was about to ask him where Doc Fletcher was when she saw the doctor coming down the stairs from his office over the barber shop, a towheaded youngster hurrying down ahead of him.

As usual, it was difficult, if not impossible, for Joanne to tell if the doctor was drunk. He was a tall, spare man with gaunt, prominent cheekbones and eyes that seemed to be looking out at the world from the depths of an ancient despair. He drank prodigiously, it was said, but seldom staggered or slurred a word — or hurt a patient that did not deserve to be hurt.

As the doctor stepped off the board walk to approach her, Joanne saw Tim Landon hurry out of his law office and push through the crowd toward her. He arrived at the wagon at about the same time the doctor did, but she ignored him as she addressed the older man.

"I've got two dead men in this wagon, Doc."

The tall man nodded, as casually as if she had just told him she had a slight cold, then let his eyes glance past her at the two bodies. He was the county coroner and would have to see to the death certificates, while the barber tended to the burying. Doc Fletcher brushed his yellowing mustache with a long forefinger and looked back at Joanne, the hint of a question in his eyes.

"It's not the greaser, Doc," she told him. "It's Pete Bushnell and Johnny Lomax. Some gunslick the greaser hired killed them."

She spoke with deliberate softness, but enough of what she said carried to the crowd. At once the front ranks broke as individuals set off to spread the word. Joanne ignored the commotion as best she could.

"The Double B will see to the funeral expenses, Doc," she went on, "if you and Burnside would please take these bodies for me. I have to go find Carol Bushnell."

At that moment Marshal Brad Borrmann hustled through the crowd, his ample gut cutting a wide swath as he moved. Tim Landon was about to say something to Joanne until he saw Borrmann. He stepped back out of the lawman's way.

"How'd it happen, Miss Beecher?"

the marshal boomed.

"Not here, Marshal," she snapped. "And not until I speak to Carol Bushnell. I'll see you in your office later."

As she climbed down from her seat, Tim Landon reached out and took her hand to assist her. She snatched her hand out of his grasp, her face instantly scarlet.

"Take your hands off me, Tim Landon," she said, her voice low but trembling with fury. "It's your fault. All of this. Pete Bushnell and Johnny Lomax would be alive now if you hadn't prevented us from hanging that murderer. Their blood is on your hands!"

Her voice carried far and the crowd was hushed as every man and woman in it strained to catch each word. Tim stepped back as if she had struck him. She could see that he had not been prepared for her outburst and was pleased she had been able to show him how she felt in this public a manner.

As she started past Tim, she paused just long enough to tell him, "Your chances in this county are gone, Mr. Landon. You'll get no further business from Double B or any of the other ranchers. And Judge Prentiss is only one more elected official. You can tell him that. Double B will handle the justice in this county from now on — the way men are supposed to handle it."

"That's telling him!" shouted someone in the crowd. At once, more than a few yelled their agreement.

Joanne paid no attention to them as she brushed past the marshal and mounted the board walk. Carol Bushnell was clerking at the hardware store in place of her husband. Joanne wanted to get to her before anyone else did.

As she passed the hotel porch, she caught sight of a tall fellow standing apart from the other guests. For only a moment she was reminded of Jed. The stranger was as tall and just as rangy, and he had the same broad brow and wide mouth. But there the resemblance ended. Unlike Jed, this fellow's eyes were an icy-blue and they held her with a bold, accusing stare.

Oddly troubled, she swept on past the hotel to the hardware store. The moment she entered the place she saw that she was not to be the first one to tell Carol of her husband. Carol was huddled in the corner, two older women with her. She looked as lost and as frightened as a little girl. When Joanne saw that look she remembered with a sharp pang her own recent loss.

With a tiny cry she ran to Carol, and as the two embraced, the older women wondered for a moment who was comforting whom.

\* \* \*

Tim Landon watched Joanne disappear into her father's store. He was standing on the board walk in front of his office, feeling not only a profound sense of loss but also a real admiration for the spunk that had drawn him to the girl from the beginning — that and her undeniable beauty, of course.

He did not like to think that there would be no softening in her attitude. For a while they had been quite close — Johnny, Joanne and himself. Apart from what this would mean in terms of the job he had yet to perform in this county, he was upset at the loss of that friendship — and the comfort it had given him.

Tim turned and started into his office, then caught himself in the doorway, turned and walked on down to the Front Street Hotel. He needed a drink, he decided — and he also needed to know what was going on. A man didn't find that out, he had long since realized, sitting in an empty law office.

A momentary hush fell over the saloon as Tim shouldered through the batwings. Tim paid it no heed as he walked quickly over to the bar and nodded his usual greeting to the hotel's barkeep.

"Whiskey," he told Sam.

The conversation started up again as Tim pulled his shot glass toward him a moment later. He turned around to face the narrow, smoke-filled room and sipped his drink thoughtfully. He met no eyes. Through long practice he had taught himself how to come into this place and not seem to pick out any one individual as he looked casually around. It was better that way. No one had to look quickly away — or stare truculently back at him to show his contempt.

Tim emptied his glass, turned back to Sam and asked for the bottle, then took it over to an empty table in the corner. He sat down with his back to the wall, facing the door and most of the faro and poker games in progress. As he had hoped, he soon became part of the furniture. The talk rose in volume and Tim listened as he poured and drank sparingly.

Sheriff Clay Allison, it seemed, had tried to take in Jose Ramirez after one of the Double B cowpokes had found a side of beef hanging in the Ramirez barn. The brand on the discarded hide was Double B, of course. It was preposterous on the face of it — that Ramirez would allow anything as incriminating as a Double B steer to hang in his barn while he and his wife went shopping in Cody — but it had been enough for Beecher to set Allison and his dogs loose on Ramirez.

What precisely had happened from then on, Tim was unable to piece together from the scraps of conversation that came to him in the crowded saloon. It was obvious, however, from what Joanne had said to him outside, that a friend of Jose's had somehow managed to help Jose escape Allison's posse, killing young Bushnell and Johnny Lomax in the process.

Tim soon noticed how the stories and speculations were beginning to repeat themselves and was about to leave when Marshal Borrmann burst into the saloon, Clay Allison and his Texans right behind him. Borrmann was elated as he marched up to the bar and slammed a fat hand down on the bar.

"Drinks on me, boys!" he cried. "The Mex is dead — and so is his squaw!"

With a rush, the saloon's patrons left their chairs and swarmed up to the bar. Tim stayed where he was, a shocked sense of outrage numbing him. Jose dead! And Mary, too! And these men were *celebrating* it.

Only one other man in the place had kept to his chair. He was sitting in the farthest corner from Tim, well to the right of the door. Tim had noticed him enter not long after he himself had sat down.

Looking at him more closely now, Tim found him to be a man that seemed tall even while sitting down. He had strong, rawboned features and eyes so light blue that as the man sat in the gloom of the corner they almost seemed to glow — like a cat's.

But it was not this fellow in the far corner that Marshal Borrmann noticed. With a foaming stein of beer held high in his right hand, he turned to face Tim. The rest of the gang at the bar followed his example.

"Well, now. Ain't you going to drink with us, Counselor?" Borrmann asked, his voice laced with insolence. "This time justice was done — with none of your fancy talk to hold it back."

The loud, brutal comments echoing that sentiment fell upon Tim with the force of something tangible. Only truly ignorant men, he realized, could be this wrong. This triumphantly wrong.

Tim shook his head and looked down at his hand. He was surprised to see that it was trembling as it held the shot glass he had been drinking from. He was ashamed of the fear and dismay he felt, and when he looked back up he saw Borrmann start along the bar toward him, his eyes angry slits.

"Damn it, Counselor," Borrmann said, slapping his glass of beer down onto the bar. "You'll drink with us — or else!"

Tim shook his head emphatically. "I'd sooner drink with murderers," he told the advancing town marshal. "In fact, that's just what I'd be doing." He looked beyond Borrmann at the other men still bellied up to the bar. "And that's what you men are doing," he told them. "You're drinking with the murderers of Jose Ramirez and his wife."

By that time Borrmann had reached Tim's table. His huge ham of a hand shot down and grabbed Tim by the front of his vest and hauled him out of his seat, upsetting the table and knocking Tim's bottle and glass to the floor.

"You ain't in no courtroom now, Landon," Borrmann said. "And they ain't no judge ready to shut me up neither. So when you call Sheriff Allison and his lawful appointed deputies murderers, I call that disturbin' the peace.''

The man brought his fist around with swift precision. Tim tried to duck back. But he was not quick enough as Borrmann's big fist caught him on his right cheek close in under the eye. Tim felt himself spinning wildly and the floor struck him in the back with surprising suddenness. He shook his head to clear it. Borrmann stepped back to wait for him to get up. There was a happy smile on Borrmann's stupid face, and at sight of that vacant grin, a wildness erupted in Tim. He scrambled quickly to his feet and flung himself at the marshal.

Tim was a slightly built man, at least half a foot shorter than Borrmann and in no sense of the word a match for the bigger, wilier brawler. Yet the enthusiasm with which Tim flung himself at the marshal startled Borrmann and caught him off-guard. Lashing out furiously, Tim caught the marshal on the side of the neck with a wild, roundhouse right, then continued after him with a punch into Borrmann's enormous midsection, following up this astonishing flurry with a looping blow to the side of the marshal's face — all of which brought a surprised cheer from the men at the bar.

But Borrmann absorbed all this with disheartening ease, and stung by the cheer from the bar, he closed with Tim and began punishing him with solid, measured blows that drove Tim back relentlessly. When Tim brought up his hands to protect his face, Borrmann would drive sledging blows to Tim's midsection until in desperation Tim rushed the man. Borrmann stepped easily inside Tim's flailing punches and countered with two solid one-two punches — one to Tim's head, the other to his face. This last punch caught Tim flush on the side of his jaw.

The room spun and Tim felt the floor slam up into him again. He blinked groggily and found himself staring at a pair of worn boots — the marshal's. As he tried to get up, one of the boots was pulled back, then sent rushing at him, catching Tim on the side of the head, just above his ear. Lights exploded deep within his skull and he felt his head crunch sharply back against the leg of a chair.

Tim reached out to grab something so that he could pull himself back up onto his feet and heard someone say, "Leave him, Brad. It's my turn now."

Tim shook himself and saw Rick Warner approaching, the man's lank blond hair partially obscuring his slack face. He was grinning at the prospect of getting his licks in.

Borrmann backed off. "Sure. Finish him for me, Rick. You heard him. He called you and Clay murderers."

"You . . . *are!*" Tim cried at them, surprised at the weak, rasping quality to his voice and aware for the first time how painful it was for him to move his lower jaw. And he had the odd feeling that his lips had doubled in size.

With a happy snarl, Rick Warner reached down and hauled Tim to his feet.

\* \* \*

Kyle had been watching warily, hoping he would be able to stay out of it. He had planned to keep out of sight, with his eyes and ears open until he got a chance to speak to Landon.

But he'd seen enough. The moment this same blond hardcase he had struck down outside Jose's cabin yanked the lawyer to his feet, he pushed himself erect and called sharply across the saloon.

"Put that fellow down gently in one of those chairs, mister. And do it now."

The blond fellow paused. He blinked, as if he were having difficulty comprehending the order.

Kyle spoke again, trying to make his tone more reasonable: "If you lay a hand on that man, it just might *be* murder. Can't you see he's already hurt bad?"

The blond's face went scarlet. He flung the lawyer from him carelessly and spun to face Kyle. "Who the hell're you, buttin' in?"

"Hey, Rick," someone from the bar called. "That sonofabitch didn't join us at the bar neither."

"That's right, I didn't," said Kyle, looking straight at the man who had spoken out. "I don't drink with the kind of official that would stand by and watch a man beaten to death without raising a hand."

"So you're raising a hand, is that it?" asked Rick, his gun hand drifting back toward the handle of his six-gun.

"That's right," said Kyle, setting himself.

Abruptly the sheriff — a tall, heavily built man in his forties with dark, blazing eyes and almost snow-white hair — stepped quickly away from the bar and placed himself between Rick and Kyle. Kyle had been about to draw, as had the blond. But now both relaxed as the sheriff turned to Kyle and spoke.

"Guess you got a point there, stranger. The counselor's had enough this time, looks like."

Then the sheriff swung around to face the blond. "Too bad, Rick. Next time you can go first. How's that?"

There was a cutting sarcasm in his tone. Kyle saw the blond slump, as if the man had been a dog his master had just scolded. Rick looked uncertainly back at Kyle, then shrugged and returned to the bar.

The sheriff looked back at Kyle. "This man a friend of yours, is he?"

"Never saw him before today."

"I see. Well, he's your friend now. Get him out of here. This here's a cattleman's bar. It ain't no proper place for him — or for you, neither. So hurry it up. The counselor's beginning to stink up the place."

There was appreciative laughter at this. Kyle felt the blood rushing into his face. This sheriff, he now realized, was the same one who had led that posse to Jose's cabin. Knowing this made it difficult for Kyle to keep his feelings under control. The important thing at the moment, however, was to get this beaten fellow to some kind of help, to the doctor he had seen outside talking to the Beecher girl, perhaps.

He walked quickly over to the lawyer and went down on one knee beside him. The man's eyes were open but unfocused, and he was trying feebly to reach up and grab the seat of a chair. When the blond they called Rick had flung him down, the lawyer's head had struck the edge of the table a mean crack. The fellow now seemed to be having difficulty in orienting himself. A thin trickle of blood was flowing steadily from his left nostril.

Reaching under the man, Kyle lifted him in his arms as easily as if he were lifting a child. Indeed, Kyle was astonished at how slightly built the lawyer was. His foolhardy courage in speaking his mind seemed to be in direct proportion to his lack of weight. Kyle started from the saloon and was halfway across the room when the Beecher girl burst into the place.

So intent was she on singling the sheriff out at the bar, she did not appear to notice Kyle and his burden on her first glance around the saloon's smoky interior. "Sheriff," she demanded. "What's this I hear about that greaser? Someone said you found his grave."

Turning to face her, the sheriff rested his back against the bar, his beer glass still in his hand. "That's right, Miss Beecher," he said. "We found where him and his wife was buried. Near that abandoned line shack on Snow Ridge."

"You're sure it was him?"

"We followed the tracks of that sonofabitch who fired on us yesterday. They led to the line shack and from there to the two graves. Whoever dug 'em put neat crosses on each one. Jose was carved on one cross and Mary on the other."

"You can rest easy now, Miss Beecher," said a tall dark fellow with a fearful welt on the side of his face.

The Beecher girl looked at his swollen face for a moment. "Yes, Frenchie. I guess I can."

She started to leave then, but as she turned her eyes caught sight of Kyle. He had stopped at her entrance, then started up again when he saw she was through with the sheriff.

"Pardon me, ma'am," he said, moving past her.

The girl took one look at the beaten man in Kyle's arms and spun to the men at the bar. "Which one of you did that?" she demanded. "Or did all of you join in?"

"I cannot tell a lie, Miss Beecher," Borrmann said, grinning foolishly at her.

"I did it with my own two hands."

"He used his foot too, ma'am," someone at the end of the bar said with a snigger.

"Rick wanted to help me out after I got tired of beating on him," Borrmann went on, apparently unaware of the girl's growing anger. "But then this stranger butted in."

"What's the matter, Miss Beecher?" drawled Rick. He had not missed the dismay reflected in the Beecher girl's face. "Hell, you should be mighty pleased with us. We got that greaser for you, and now Brad here's wiped up the floor with that fool lawyer what got the Mex off in the first place."

"Yes," she told the blond fellow coldly. "I am pleased that the man who killed my brother and rustled Double B cattle is dead. But I don't remember sicking any of you on Tim Landon."

"You sure got a short memory," protested Borrmann. "All of us heard what you told the counselor outside. You really laid into him. The whole town heard what you said to him."

Kyle had reached the door by this time. As he pushed through the batwings, he heard the girl marching angrily out after him. He was just beyond the hotel entrance when she overtook him.

"Bring Tim to Doctor Fletcher," she told Kyle curtly. "Follow me."

Without a word, Kyle shifted his now unconscious burden slightly and followed the girl along the board walk and then up the outside stairway to the doctor's second-floor office over the barber shop. Inside, Kyle found a small waiting room with the doctor's consulting room further in. Beyond that, Kyle saw, was a long room with four or five cots along one wall.

The doctor poked his head out of the office and took in Kyle's burden at a glance. "In here," he told Kyle, moving ahead of them into the long room with the cots.

The doctor waited by the first cot, his long cadaverous face assuming a weary cast. Kyle put Landon down as gently as he could and stepped back.

"Who did this?" the doctor asked, his fingers probing the lawyer's face expertly, gently.

"I'll let Miss Beecher explain," Kyle said.

The doctor leaned close to Landon and examined the man's eyes. "Let's have it, Joanne," he said, without looking up.

Joanne glanced resentfully at Kyle, then squared her shoulders and told the doctor what she had learned in the saloon. Finishing up, she glanced with tight lips at Kyle and said, "This gentleman was there at the time. He was not much help, evidently."

"That's right, Miss," Kyle admitted. "But I did stop it when that blond fellow moved in to take up where the town marshal left off."

"You stood up to Rick Warner?" she asked, grudging respect evident in her voice.

"That sheriff, he sort of sided with me."

She frowned. "You mean Clay Allison, do you? I'm surprised he showed that much sense." Then she looked at Tim. "Borrmann's an animal," she said. "I despise him. Clay Allison and his Texans, as well."

The doctor was wiping blood from Tim Landon's nostrils. He glanced up at the girl. "Each one of them animals is in your employ, Miss Beecher — you and your father's, that is."

"We have no choice," she snapped. "It's either that or have our ranges rustled clean."

Landon groaned and stirred suddenly. As he started to raise himself, the doctor gently restrained him. Landon opened his eyes and tried to focus on the doctor.

"You've got a concussion, Landon," the doctor told him, "and maybe a broken rib or two. You just lie still there. And that's an order."

Squinting, Landon looked past the doctor at Kyle and Joanne. He smiled slightly when he saw Joanne, then frowned quickly as if the smile had cost him. He looked back at the doctor.

"I got an awful headache, Doctor," he said.

"You should see your face," said the doctor in response. "If you feel as bad as you look, you'd just better lie still. Hear?"

Landon nodded ever so slightly and closed his eyes. The doctor pulled an army blanket up around him and, beckoning to them, led them out of the room. He closed the door softly, then turned to them.

"After he's got some rest and his headache lets up, I'll bind up those ribs of his." He shook his head and frowned slightly. "He should be all right in a couple of weeks, depending on just how serious that head injury is." He looked sharply at Kyle. "There is a welt just above his temple. Looks like he was kicked."

Kyle nodded. "Borrmann caught him with his boot on the side of the head — when he was on the floor."

The doctor shook his head. "Well, it missed the temple and that does not appear to be where the damage was done."

"I think he hit the back of his head, Doctor, when Rick flung him to the floor."

"That might be it, then." Fletcher pulled out one of his desk drawers, lifted a fifth of whiskey and a shot glass out of it and proceeded to pour himself two fingers. "We'll just have to wait and see. At least our brand of corrupt lawman doesn't try to pretend he's anything other than what he is — a brute and a bully." The doctor downed his whiskey and looked wearily at Joanne. "This, young lady, is an example of the kind of local justice you so applauded less than an hour ago."

"It doesn't alter the facts, Doctor," Joanne said, stung by his words. "My brother died at the hands of a man this lawyer helped wriggle out of a rope." Then her face softened somewhat. "But that part of it is finished now. Jose Ramirez is dead. And the Double B is intact. In the end, Doctor, that is all that really matters. That is what Jed lived — and died — for."

"Yes," he said, shaking his head at the absurdity of it. "I suppose it is."

Joanne Beecher looked at Kyle. Kyle had been watching her closely, aware that this woman — and her father, according to what little Jose was able to tell him —

was the driving force behind Jose's death.

"You're a stranger in Cody, mister," she said. "What's your name?"

"Kyle," he replied. "Kyle Robinson."

"I don't suppose you realized it, but when you went against Rick Warner and the others, you bought yourself a peck of trouble."

"I wasn't thinking about that at the time."

She frowned. "No, of course you weren't," she admitted. "Are you planning on staying on in these parts?"

"I was thinking of it."

She glanced at the closed door that hid the beaten man from her, then looked back up at Kyle. It was obvious she felt she owed Kyle something. "Well, I like a man who's not unwilling to stand up to those men. We're short-handed at the Double B. You look like you've worked cows before."

"Just about all my life," Kyle admitted.

"Good. Ride out to Double B tomorrow and we'll sign you on. Thirty dollars a month and found."

"I don't remember asking for a job,"

Kyle replied softly.

Joanne blushed and her dark eyes snapped impatiently. "The Double B is the largest spread in this territory. And we take care of our riders. If you plan on working in this county, you couldn't find a better spread to work on — or a safer one."

"Is that a threat, Miss Beecher?"

"Of course not," she snapped. "It's a fact."

"Well, thank you, Miss Beecher. I appreciate the offer, but I've already got a place. My own spread."

She frowned. "Your own?"

"The J Bar."

"The J — !"

"That's right, Miss Beecher. Only I guess I'll be changing the brand to the K Bar now, since Jose's dead."

She took a step backward, her face white.

"I'm half owner, Miss Beecher. We both put in an equal amount when we bought the place. I have my copy of the deed." He touched the brim of his hat. "But I thank you for the offer, Miss Beecher."

Then he glanced at the doctor. There

was for just a moment a glint of amusement in the man's long face. "I'll be in to see. Mr. Landon later, Doc. Take good care of him."

"'I'll do that, Mr. Robinson."

Kyle nodded curtly to Joanne Beecher. Her face was dark now with fury. She was, of course, connecting him with the death of two of her people and the sniper that made her leap unceremoniously from her wagon seat into Jose's cabin.

"Just a moment, Mr. Robinson," she said coldly.

Kyle, in the act of opening the door, paused and looked back at the girl. "Yes, Miss Beecher?"

"If you're the one who —"

"Miss Beecher, I don't know what you're talking about. I just arrived in town this afternoon."

He smiled then, coldly.

"You deny that you're the one who shot and killed Johnny Lomax and Pete Bushnell?"

"Yes, Miss Beecher. Of course I do. Just as you will deny having anything to do with the murder of Mary Ramirez and her husband, Jose." Kyle was no longer smiling. "You said a little while ago that that part of it was finished. It isn't, Miss Beecher. And it won't be until all those who took part in that ugly business pay for their part in it."

He pulled the door open and glanced back.

"I said *all,* Miss Beecher."

He closed the door and started down the long stairway to the street.

# 4

As Kyle sank into a wicker chair on the hotel porch a few moments later and built himself a smoke, he chided himself mildly for having told the Beecher girl as much as he had. But he consoled himself with the knowledge that she would have known about him soon enough.

When he arrived in Cody earlier that day, he had gone straight to the land office to get a copy of the deed Jose and he had obtained for their 160-acre homestead claim along the stream, and to make certain it was recorded properly. It was, and as the only surviving partner, the ranch was now his. He also found that the three small ranches that had stood between J Bar and Beecher's Double B spread were no longer on the maps. They had either been bought out or abandoned. The J Bar was now the only ranch that stood between the

Double B and the Sweetwater range —
which Double B now claimed.

In each case, the land agent told Kyle,
the adjoining ranchers had been caught
rustling Double B stock or had had their
own cattle rustled. Could Double B be
rustling its own stock as an excuse to go
after the small ranchers? It *was* possible,
Kyle realized — until he thought of Joanne
Beecher. Obviously, she was very much a
part of Double B's operation, and though
she was strong-willed and tragically
wrongheaded when it came to Jose, she
was honest. His brief dealings with her had
convinced him of that. And then there was
the death of her brother. How could that
possibly fit into such a scheme?

No. There had to be some other
explanation. And that meant that Kyle's
first task would be to find those
responsible for rustling Double B cattle
and framing Jose for it.

His reflections were interrupted by the
sight of Joanne Beecher hurrying past the
hotel porch and entering the hotel saloon.
A moment later she left the place and
walked swiftly past the porch in the other

direction. As Kyle watched her go, he noted with a grim smile how the girl could not seem to resist a quick, vengeful glance in his direction. Kyle flicked away his smoke and waited.

Not long after, he saw her leaving town driving the same flatbed wagon she had used to bring in the two dead men. Beside her on the seat was a woman of about her age wearing a black dress and bonnet, her face white and drawn. Kyle guessed it was a widow or relation to one of the men Joanne had brought in.

It was not until the dust had settled completely after the wagon's passage that the three Texans and Marshal Borrmann left the hotel saloon and mounted the porch where Kyle was sitting. Kyle leaned his chair back so that it was resting against the side of the hotel.

As the four men approached, Kyle saw the other loungers on the porch get hastily to their feet and clear off it. Even across the street, those townspeople who saw what was afoot were beginning to move for cover. Kyle had little difficulty in imagining the speed with which Joanne

Beecher's information about Kyle must have sped down Front Street.

The four men came to a halt in front of Kyle. He met their gaze evenly, glad suddenly that he was openly face-to-face with the last three of those butchers who had killed Jose and Mary. He did not yet know what part Marshal Borrmann had played in that business, but he was willing to bet his role in it would become apparent soon enough.

Kyle had recognized earlier in the saloon the two men he had struck unconscious beside their campfire. The ugly welt on the face of the one Kyle had heard the Beecher girl call Frenchie appeared much more painful in the bright sunlight. And the blond, Rick Warner, was rocking uncertainly on his feet, his eyes blinking painfully as he peered with barely suppressed fury at Kyle.

"What's your name, mister?" the sheriff asked.

"Kyle Robinson. Didn't Miss Beecher tell you?"

"Sure. She told us. You're the sonofabitch that shot us up yesterday.

You killed Pete Bushnell and Johnny."

"You got witnesses?"

"You deny it?"

"I asked if you got witnesses."

"You don't deny it, then."

"Let me at the sonofabitch," said Frenchie to the sheriff.

Allison reached out his left hand and prevented Frenchie from moving closer to Kyle. "The sonofabitch is right. We don't have no witnesses."

"I'll swear to it," said Frenchie. "That's the guy that slugged me and Rick. I'll swear to it, Clay."

Kyle slipped his holster around casually so that it rested on top of his right thigh, the six-gun inside it pointed directly at the sheriff. "You'd have to take me in, Sheriff," Kyle said quietly. "And if I am who you think I am, I'd think twice if I were you about giving me such a sweet chance to finish what you say I've already started."

"You'd never get all four of us."

"Perhaps not. But I'll get you first. And that's a promise."

"You'd be resisting arrest."

"Where's your warrant, Sheriff?"

"I'll get one."

"Get it," Kyle said, smiling. "Then serve it."

"Just a moment here!"

Kyle glanced past the sheriff. A tall, formidable gentleman in a derby hat and a long frock coat was approaching the porch from across the street. And keeping step with him were the doctor and two grim-looking townsmen. As the four men approached, townspeople eased themselves out of doorways and began to crowd closer to the hotel porch.

Clay Allison swung around to face the fellow in the derby hat. "We don't need you, Judge."

"Yes, you do," the man said, mounting the porch steps. "If you're talking about warrants, you do."

Frenchie spoke up heatedly. "Now, listen here, Judge! This here gent shot Pete Bushnell and Johnny Lomax! And he beat up me and Rick outside the greaser's cabin!"

The judge's eyebrows went up a notch. "Indeed? Is that the cabin where you besieged Ramirez and his wife? As I understand from the doctor here, both are dead now. And each one of you had a hand in that ugly business."

"Ramirez resisted arrest, Judge," said Clay Allison.

"And his wife?"

"That was an accident, Judge. We was after Jose."

"I don't remember issuing any warrant for the arrest of Jose Ramirez, Sheriff."

"We were just bringing him in for questioning."

"Of course you were," the judge said, his voice laced with sarcasm. The judge looked at Frenchie. "Tell me about it, Frenchie."

"We was sitting around the campfire when this guy knocked out Rick. I turned and he hit me with the barrel of his six-gun."

"You mentioned campfire, Frenchie. Was it night?"

Frenchie frowned and looked helplessly at the sheriff. Then he looked back at the judge and nodded.

"And did it happen quickly?"

Again Frenchie nodded.

"And Rick was unconscious by this time?"

"Yeah. That's right."

"So you are identifying a man you saw only for a second or two in the darkness and you have no witness to corroborate your testimony."

"To *what*, Judge?"

"To back up your story."

"I know what I saw, Judge."

The judge looked at the sheriff. "Your Texans can swear to anything they like, Allison. But I don't have to believe them. Jose Ramirez and his wife are dead. And Tim Landon is close to death right now in the doctor's office. That tells me enough about your capacity for keeping the peace. I've already sent a telegram to the territorial governor."

The judge looked at Kyle then, his keen gray eyes looking deep into Kyle's. "Young man, the law around here looks pretty sick right now. But if I were you, I'd give it a little more time."

Then the judge turned to Borrmann. "The town council is meeting this afternoon, Marshal. Despite Beecher's vote, we have already got enough votes to take your badge when the meeting is concluded. I suggest you give it to me now — just to save me a trip over to your office later."

Borrmann paled and glanced at Allison. But there was no help from that quarter. With a snarl, Borrmann ripped the badge from his vest and flung it at the judge's feet.

With this show of contempt, Borrmann spun on his heels and led the sheriff and his two deputies off the porch. Their horses were at the tie rail in front of the hotel saloon. In a moment the four men were mounted and charging out of town toward North Pass — and the Double B.

When they had gone Kyle rocked his chair forward, bent and picked up the badge and handed it to the judge, standing up as he did so. The judge took it and looked up at Kyle.

"Your name is Kyle Robinson, I take it," the man said.

Kyle nodded.

"I'm Judge Prescott. The doctor here

told me about you standing up to those men earlier — and standing up to Joanne Beecher as well. He also said you plan on taking over the J Bar — that you and Jose Ramirez were partners.''

''That's right, Judge. But I was real silent. I just helped Jose with the purchase and with stocking the place. I figured maybe I'd need a place to rest my bones someday when I got tired of punching other men's cows. So I guess that time's come.''

The judge's hand shot out. ''You'll need luck,'' the judge told Kyle grimly as Kyle took the man's strong hand and shook it. ''And all the sand you can muster. I won't be the judge here much longer if Beecher has his way. But while I'm here you can count on me.''

''Thank you, Judge.''

The tall, flinty old man looked shrewdly at Kyle. ''But only as long as you keep on the right side of the law, young man. I want you to remember that. I know how you must feel about what happened to Jose and his wife. However, I'll not countenance anyone taking the law into his own hands. We've had enough of that already." The man's eyes went hard. "If you ignore that advice, Kyle Robinson, you'll get no support from me."

"Okay, Judge."

"Fine."

The man turned then and marched off the porch, the doctor and the townsmen going with him. Kyle watched them go, then looked about him at the other townspeople still staring at him. He touched the brim of his hat to them and started off the porch on his way to the blacksmith's shop. If the K Bar was now his brand, he'd need an iron that said just that.

And once he had his own brand, he could begin rounding up the J Bar cattle the Double B hands must have let drift onto their land. And if there was trouble, well, there was no way he could run from that.

\* \* \*

Carl Beecher was furious. Joanne had never seen her father this angry.

Borrmann was standing sheepishly in front of her father's desk. Clay Allison, smoking a cheroot, had made himself comfortable as usual in the big leather armchair to one side. Frenchie and Rick were leaning against the wall behind Clay. Joanne was sitting on the sofa, watching Borrmann and her father.

It had been bad enough when she had ridden in with Carol Bushnell and told her father about Kyle Robinson and what Borrmann had done to Tim Landon. But what Borrmann had just said seemed to have been the last straw for her father.

"You let that judge take away your badge?" her father asked Borrmann again. "You didn't demand a hearing before the town council? You just let him take it?"

Borrmann tried to bluster. "When he said he had enough votes in the council, I just threw the badge at him. I don't need that piece of tin."

"You fool! You're not the one that needs it! I'm the one. As long as I owned you and you had that badge, whatever I did in that town was legal!"

Borrmann shifted unhappily before Joanne's father. "Mr. Beecher, you didn't own me."

"Like hell I didn't! It was my votes that got you that job. It was my votes that kept you on, no matter how much you drank or who you beat up. But turning on that lawyer like that lost me what votes I had on the council. It'll be twice as hard now for me to get rid of that old fool Prescott."

Borrmann started to frame a reply, but lost heart before he got a word out. He looked miserably over to Clay Allison for support, but Allison, Joanne noted ironically, became intensely interested in the end of his cheroot.

"Get out of here!" her father said to Borrmann in disgust. "You too, Frenchie — Rick. Go see cookie if you're hungry. You're welcome to sleep in the bunkhouse tonight. Now just get out."

Borrmann clapped his hat back on and shuffled unhappily out of the big room, Frenchie and Rick following. When they were gone, Joanne's father looked over at Allison.

"I don't like it," he told the sheriff. "We've got a new territorial governor. I don't know the man. And it sounds to me like Prescott does."

"Or thinks he does."

"No matter. Beating up a county prosecutor sure as hell is not the way for a town marshal to behave. And you were on hand throughout the thrashing, Clay. What the hell were you thinking of?"

"Sorry, Carl," the black-eyed Texan drawled. "But I enjoyed every minute of it. That man called us all murderers. Like Borrmann said, if that's not disturbing the peace, I'd sure as hell like to know what is. He was libeling all of us — for seeing justice done to that rustling greaser."

Joanne felt the blood rushing into her face, and before she could hold herself in, she was clearing her voice angrily. Both men turned to face her. "I don't think anything Tim said could possibly have been enough of an excuse to beat him like that," she said, surprised at the emotion in her voice. But the words kept tumbling out. "Tim is not a big man. Borrmann is a brute." She found herself on her feet, looking furiously at Clay Allison. "Is that the way it is done in Texas, Mr. Allison?"

The Texan's eyes went hard. She could see the blood draining from his face and realised with pleasure that she had struck a vital spot with that last remark. From the moment this man and his sidekicks had arrived from Texas, she and her father had seen nothing but trouble. Clay Allison was bad luck for Double B, and she would see her father later this day to demand that Allison and his entire crew be sent back to Texas where they belonged.

"Joanne," her father said wearily, "that remark was uncalled for. During all our trouble, it has been Clay who has stuck by our side. He came a long way to help us. It was a mistake for him to let Landon get beaten up like that, but you must admit that Tim certainly asked for trouble. And from what I hear, you were not very kind to the man yourself this afternoon."

Before Joanne could respond, Allison spoke up. "Landon will soon be up and around — and none the worse for wear, Miss Beecher." His dark eyes went cold then and he glanced at her father. "And maybe next time he'll be a little more careful where he drinks."

Joanne glanced at her father. She could tell he was unwilling to continue the argument and was getting impatient. "Joanne," he said wearily, "think of it this way. We can all be grateful, at least, that Jose Ramirez will no longer be picking our ranges clean. And his death will serve as a warning to others. At least, that much we've gained."

But she was not satisfied, not at all. Still, she knew there was nothing more she could say. "I'll speak to you later, Father," she said.

Joanne got up then and left the room. Without having to guide her footsteps, she found herself in what had been Jed's bedroom and office combined. She slumped, utterly drained, into his big wing chair by the window and tried to sort out her feelings.

All she had wanted, she had thought, was the death of that Mexican. And yet, the moment she saw Tim Landon's battered face, the rage that had fired her these past terrible weeks had drained from her. From that moment on she had felt only confusion — that and a dismal emptiness. Now the memory of that confrontation with Kyle Robinson so soon after filled her with a deep sense of unease.

It seemed that no matter what they did, no matter how many ranchers or nesters they fought off, others would always appear on their flanks to harry them still. Her father's response when she repeated Kyle Robinson's threat had not seemed at all appropriate. He had laughed, dismissing the man almost casually, saying that all the fellow had accomplished in coming here was to find a good spot to bury his friend.

And this despite the fact that Robinson had already killed two of their own men.

She leaned back in the chair and looked out through the window at the lush coverlet of grassland that swept all the way to the peaks of the Wind River Range, the mighty capped battlement that protected their valley. It was a scene Jed had loved. It was why he had chosen this room for himself.

But now Jed was gone. And above Joanne in this big lonely house Carol Bushnell was in her room, weeping for the loss of her husband — while she sat down here in this big chair watching the lengthening shadows fall across the range, bracing herself for whatever new trouble this implacable stranger with the cold-blue eyes was destined to bring to the Double B . . .

\* \* \*

Sheriff Clay Allison poked at Frenchie impatiently in the darkness of the bunkhouse. It took a while for him to get much of a response out of Frenchie, so weary was the man — and that Allison understood completely. He was just as exhausted.

"What is it?" protested Frenchie.

"Get up and meet me outside. Don't wake any of Beecher's hands, but get Rick and Brad too."

Frenchie mumbled something unintelligible, then flicked his blanket off and sat up on his bunk, scratching the top of his head sleepily. Allison didn't wait for any argument. He went outside and waited by the lodgepole corral.

In a few minutes the three men padded on bare feet out of the bunkhouse and caught sight of him. The three of them were wearing long johns and in the bright moonlight looked like comic apparitions as they picked their way across the yard.

"What the hell is this, Clay?" Borrmann wanted to know. He was hugging himself to keep from shivering in the chill night air.

"Just got through talking to Beecher."

"What's he want?"

"He says it don't make any kind of sense. We get rid of the greaser — then let another one pop right up in his place. He's real upset."

"He's talking about this Robinson?" Frenchie asked.

"Who the hell do you think?"

"Well, damn it, Clay — he didn't seem so exercised when we told him about Robinson before."

"Hell, man. His daughter was in the

room. He didn't want her to know how he felt. It'd only worry her, he says."

"I'd like to worry her," Rick said meanly. "And I'd start off by blistering her backside. She needs to learn some manners, that bitch does."

"That's enough of that, Rick," Allison said sharply.

Rick grinned and looked around at the others. "I'm only saying what everybody here is thinking."

"Let's get on with it," said Borrmann unhappily. "It's cold out here."

"I've got to go back to Cody tonight," Allison said. "Tomorrow, Borrmann, you're clearing out — at least until the feeling about the way you beat Landon settles some. You better hope the sonofabitch doesn't die."

"He had it coming." Borrmann said.

"Who the hell is arguing with you? Just stay low at the canyon ranch until I get word to you."

Borrmann nodded sullenly.

Allison looked at Frenchie and Rick. In the moonlight he could see Frenchie's battered face, and Rick still had that dazed look he couldn't seem to shake. "How'd you two like to settle with Robinson tomorrow?"

"What you got in mind?" Frenchie asked, obviously interested.

"His cows are gone. That's for sure. But he's still got the ranchhouse, the corrals and the barn standing. He's just a fiddlefoot cowboy with some buildings and no stock. Why don't we make him a fiddlefoot cowboy with no stock and no ranch buildings either?"

"Hell, there's no trick to that, Clay," Frenchie said, nudging Rick.

"We'll burn the sonofabitch to the ground," said Rick.

Allison nodded. "I'll be in Cody, so no one can blame me — and afterward, you two can join Borrmann at the canyon ranch."

"Say, Clay," Rick said, blinking at the sheriff through the darkness, "that sonofabitch gave me an awful headache. I can't hardly sit a horse no more. I'd like to do more than just burn him out."

Allison shrugged. "Suit yourself. But do it cleanly with no one to point the finger at me or Beecher."

"How much, Clay?" Frenchie asked.

"What do you mean?"

"I mean what's in the kitty for me and Rick? After this little chore for Beecher, Rick and me, we're heading south. This country ain't to our liking. It's too high and cold."

"You don't have to worry, Frenchie. Beecher told me to be sure to take good care of you fellows."

"How much, Clay?"

"A couple of hundred to each of you."

"Only a couple a hundred?"

"You finish Robinson — clean, like I said — and it'll be five hundred apiece. And don't forget the satisfaction you'll be getting at the same time."

Frenchie looked at Rick. Rick nodded.

"All right," said Frenchie. "Five hundred apiece, in silver — and also we got a long ride ahead of us, so we want the pick of the remuda. We got us some pretty fine horseflesh at that place."

Allison nodded. "We'll settle up the day after tomorrow at the ranch. How's that?"

"Fine. Now let us get some sleep, Clay."

The three turned and made their way back across the yard and disappeared into the bunkhouse. Allison watched them go, then went back to the main house where his saddled horse was waiting by the tie rail. As he swung into the saddle, he thought of what Frenchie had said about leaving this high country for the warmth of the South.

It was too bad, he supposed, that neither of them was likely to make it south. The way Allison had it figured, he'd be bringing their bodies back to Cody for the murder of Kyle Robinson. It would make him and Beecher look good for a change, and be a hell of a lot cheaper. He was sure Beecher would approve.

Yessir, he told himself, as he guided his horse out through the gate, he had a good thing going with Beecher. If he played his cards right, with Beecher's kid dead, he just might be able to chuck this badge and take over the Double B as ramrod. And then he found himself thinking of Joanne.

He frowned. She was a bit young for him and didn't seem to care for him overmuch — but she was a lot of woman all the same. And he liked the way she stood up to him and the boys.

Of course, Rick was right. She needed to be taken down a peg. But hell, he was just the man to gentle a rambunctious filly like that.

As Allison rode on through the moonlit night, he smiled at the prospect.

# 5

Kyle was troubled and angry. Starting early that morning, he had ridden over all of Jose's land in a fruitless search for J Bar stock. After that, he had kept going and found himself on Double B land.

It had been enough to excite his wonder — and more. Having worked cattle all his life, he saw at once what Beecher had and why the rancher was willing to go to any lengths to keep it. Though Kyle tried to suppress it, he felt a deep, gut-cinching surge of envy.

For more than half a day, Kyle rode over a land as broad and spacious as an ocean. It rolled off endlessly on either side in gentle swells that merged almost imperceptibly with the great blue hills shouldering distantly against the sky. Grama grass, bluestem — even the tight, curly buffalo grass — he found everywhere. It was so thick that his horse's hooves made hardly a sound as Kyle rode across the land. Indeed, almost the only sound in Kyle's ears was the sweep of the wind as it rippled across the grass, constantly transforming its hue and its gentle contours.

And there was water too, big springs welling up, sending icy rivulets across the fields, many of them feeding eventually into the same creek that flashed past Kyle's cabin — but that now coiled lazily through these fat lands, toward the distant high bluff clad with juniper and pine that backed the Double B's ranchhouse.

He had topped a gentle rise early that afternoon and found himself looking down upon the big hacienda. It was a massive building painted a white stucco over adobe, with red-tile roofs and a series of smaller barns and outbuildings clustered about it, the whole business nestled within a grove of giant old cottonwoods.

He sat his horse awhile, taking it all in; then he turned back to the mountains and his high valley. Throughout his ride, however, he had seen surprisingly few cattle. Indeed, the grass was perhaps too lush, too tall. The few bunches of crossbred longhorn-Herefords he had come across were doing fine. They were almost staggering under the weight of their beef and tallow. All were without doubt Double B stock, but they were few and far between. And there was no sign — none at all — of J Bar beef. Whoever was picking this range clean was doing a thorough job of it.

Just before sundown — still on Double B land — as Kyle was climbing into the high country, paralleling a long, high bluff, he followed a trail into an arroyo that led into a small box canyon. Like everywhere else is this lush country, the floor of the canyon was covered with horse-chest-high grama and bluestem. And in the far corner, close by a small stream, he found nearly thirty head of fat J Bar cattle.

He almost whooped with delight — until he realized how little of Jose's stock this small gather amounted to; and now as he drove his meager find onto his land, his anger returned. With all that Beecher had, how could the man possibly want more? Greed such as his was a sickness — and more. It was almost evil. And certainly only a devil could have fashioned the terror and the heartache that Kyle had witnessed these past few days . . .

He caught of the black column of smoke just before he reached the creek. The smoke was pumping furiously into the sky and the smell of burning things came to him at almost the same time. He spurred his horse through the cattle, scattering them, and crested a grassy knoll that give him an unobstructed view of his cabin on the other side of the creek.

It was almost totally consumed by the flames at this stage, the underbelly of the black plumes a bright red. Even as Kyle guided his mount down the other side of the knoll, he saw the barn explode into flames. Roweling furiously, he guided his horse across the shallow creek and loped up the far side.

The shot came as he hit the flat just below the cabin. The bullet missed him and nicked the horse's right flank. Beneath him, the horse reeled wildly. Kyle fought to stay in the saddle and buried his fist in the horse's mane. Another shot tore his hat off his head. The chin strap sawed against his Adam's apple. The horse sidestepped, twisted, and swung Kyle over to one side. Pitching headlong out of the saddle, Kyle slammed into the ground with his shoulder, then felt himself being yanked along the ground by the pull of the reins. He let go of them. The horse bolted back down the valley.

A third shot cut the grass by his head. He rolled quickly away, raised himself on one knee, stumbled, then dove back toward the creek. The next slug plowed into the back of his right shoulder and sent him headfirst down the creek embankment. Shaking his head, he found he had a mouthful of dirt. He swung around, took out his six-gun and flung himself up the embankment, ignoring as best he could the hammering in his shoulder.

Peering over the top of the embankment, Kyle saw the two horsemen, charging down the slope leading from the barn. He recognized them both. Frenchie and his sidekick, Rick Warner. They both had their rifles out and were leaning over the necks of their horses. Kyle cocked his Peacemaker and waited, praying that the hammering in his shoulder would not spoil his aim.

He waited until he could see the individual strands of Rick Warner's stringy blond hair, then fired twice, aiming low, in hopes of stopping their horses at least. But the hunk of lead in his shoulder made it impossible for him to handle the revolver's kick. Each shot went wide. And by this time the two riders were levering their Winchesters rapidly, firing as they came. Their withering fusillade tore up the ground in front of Kyle. He had a difficult time keeping the dirt out of his eyes.

He shifted his weapon to his left hand. The two riders were filling the sky now. Thumbing the hammer of his Colt, he rolled to one side and fired upward. A great dark shape stretched across the sky and another one followed it as both horsemen crested the embankment. They had hoped to ride him down, but he had rolled away just in time.

Now he kept rolling and kept firing, scarcely aware of his thumb cocking the Peacemaker. The two riders splashed on through the creek and tried to turn in their saddles to finish him with their rifles. Kyle steadied his left hand, aimed at Frenchie and fired.

Frenchie swore, yanked his horse around and started galloping along the far side of the stream, away from Kyle. Rick Warner followed, throwing a few shots back at Kyle as he did. As Kyle watched, he saw Frenchie sag in his saddle. But Warner caught Frenchie before he could tumble off his horse. Then Frenchie managed to straighten himself, and the two riders splashed back across the stream and headed north up the valley.

His right shoulder protesting, Kyle struggled to his feet and stood there unsteadily as he watched the two men gallop out of sight. Then he turned to look for his mount. The animal had been spooked bad enough to send him boiling into the next county. Instead, the horse was standing in the middle of the flat below the creek, cropping the lush pasture. As

Kyle started toward the horse his eye was able to pick out the crimson slash the slug had left as it creased the animal's flank.

Kyle spoke softly to the horse as he got close to it. The animal's head pumped up, his ears going flat, his nostrils flaring.

"Come on now, fella," Kyle said gently.

The horse backed, and Kyle forced a smile into his voice as he reached out for the reins with his left hand. "Easy, boy. Easy."

The horse took another step backward, his flanks quivering. Kyle lunged for the reins and managed to grab them securely as the animal reared. Kyle hung on and dug his heels into the thick carpet of grass. The horse came down, snorting.

"Easy, fella," Kyle called softly, wondering why in hell his right arm hadn't dropped off by this time.

The horse stood with all four legs locked stiffly, ears flickering, tail snapping. Without releasing his hold on the reins, Kyle reached up with his left hand and grabbed the saddle horn and pulled himself onto the saddle, then swung his right boot over the cantle into the stirrup.

By this time his right shoulder and arm was a useless, leaden addition to his body. The pain reminded him of a small and furious animal gnawing away at the bone and muscle and was something he realized he was simply going to have to ignore. But the loss of blood was beginning to tell on him. He knew this from the cold sweat that stood out just beyond his hairline and the fact that despite his recent exertion his teeth were beginning to chatter.

But his hat was back there somewhere on the ground and he did not intend to ride into Cody without any headgear. He hauled the horse around and went back for his hat.

*      *      *

Clay Allison levered a cartridge into his Winchester as Warner and Frenchie rode closer. He was perched on an outcropping of rock at least twenty feet above the trail that led through the pass. He wedged the rifle stock into his shoulder and sighted on the lead rider, Warner. His fingers sweated against the wood of the stock as he waited for Warner to get closer. Abruptly, Warner turned in his saddle and leaned quickly to one side to grab at Frenchie riding beside him.

Clay swore and lowered the Winchester. Frenchie was having a helluva time staying in his saddle. At once Allison knew that something had gone wrong. He stood up, watched the two riders a moment longer, then turned and jumped down off the rock, snatched up his horse's reins and swung into the saddle.

The rifle was in its scabbard as he cut onto the trail a few yards on the far side of the rock and started toward the two riders.

Frenchie and Warner pulled up when they saw Clay approaching. As Clay got closer, he saw that Frenchie was simply hanging on to his saddle horn. The man's dark face had lost all its color and his thin lips were compressed tightly. Rick Warner had a sullen, defiant look — so Allison expected the worst.

''Okay,'' Allison said, pulling up

alongside Warner. "What went wrong?"

Without looking up at him, Frenchie said, "I got shot. Bad."

"Where you hit?"

"My back. Low. The slug's sitting in my gut right now. Jesus Christ, Clay. I think I bought it."

"What about Robinson?"

Warner spoke up. "We burnt him out. There ain't a stick left standing. The place went up like a stack of dry hay."

"I said, what about Robinson?"

"We winged him," Warner said.

"You mean he got away."

"But not before we caught him a good one, Clay," Rick Warner said. "Jesus, just give us the money and let us get out of here. We don't want the whole shot now. Just what you promised for burning Robinson out."

"And bring me a doctor, Clay," said Frenchie.

"You want me to go into Cody and bring Doc Fletcher out here?"

"I'm hurt bad, Clay."

"So I should bring Fletcher out here to the canyon ranch. And of course he won't notice a thing. He won't notice the corrals. Anything. You know I can't do that, Frenchie."

"Just get him, Clay. I need him."

"Sure," said Warner, watching Clay closely. "We'll worry about that other after he's fixed up Frenchie. We got plenty of booze on hand. We just might be able to talk the doctor into staying with us for a while."

The look in Warner's eyes warned Allison. He decided to go along.

"I'll see what I can do," Allison said. "Maybe I can tell him one of the Double B hands fell off a horse."

"We'll be waiting on you at the canyon ranch," Warner said. "And hurry it up. Frenchie's hurt bad. We need to get that bullet out."

Allison nodded, his face grim with resolve. He was cursing himself for not having squeezed that trigger a few moments before. Rick Warner was concerned enough about Frenchie's condition to give Clay trouble. Already he was giving Clay orders.

"I'll be back as soon as I can," he told

them, and clapped spurs to his horse.

He was well down the trail before he turned in his saddle to look back. Frenchie was riding slumped over the saddle horn and Rick Warner was reaching out to steady him in the saddle as they rode. He watched them a moment longer until they disappeared into the pass.

He turned back around in his saddle, his face lit by a bleak smile. Hell, Frenchie would be dead before morning. No sense in lathering himself about it. He could forget the doctor.

But he wanted to get back to Cody on the double. He needed to know how badly Robinson was hurt — and just how much he had been able to figure out when he saw Warner and Frenchie coming after him.

\*     \*     \*

Cody's main street was quiet. The saloons were all shut down by this time and the only light came from the full moon sailing high overhead. Its light was all Kyle needed as he guided his horse down the street.

He was thinking foolish thoughts by this time, his mind full of fuzzy, tail-chasing ideas. It was almost as if he were in the middle of a high lonesome, except that he hadn't touched any firewater in the last couple of days. A puncher was suddenly expelled from a darkened saloon, but not quietly and not without a few well-chosen epithets as he picked himself up off the board walk and, leaning on a post, carefully fitted his dark Stetson down over his tousled head. He charged onto his horse and rode recklessly past Kyle and out of town.

Kyle clung to his horse the way he imagined a sailor would cleave himself to a deck in a hurricane and realized at last why they called a saddle a hurricane deck. Only this horse of his wasn't buckin' none. He was walking down the middle of the street as calm and peaceful as a well-watered steer. Kyle smiled ironically at his condition, but there was pain in the irony as well as humor.

If I can get to that doctor, he thought, and if he can dig this piece of lead out of my shoulder and if he can stop the bleeding, then maybe I can do what I promised. Maybe. An image of the girl flashed before him and he recalled his cruel words to her: *It won't be finished until all those who took part in that ugly business pay their part in it.* Was that what I said? Something like that, anyway. And I told Jose I'd get them all. Every one of them. And that included the girl, didn't it? Only now I'm having trouble stayin' in my saddle.

He felt a bleak despair all of a sudden. The weight of his promise to Jose seemed like an added burden as he rode. He became aware of the chill wind on his sweat-streaked face, of the dizziness . . . and then, as if by some kind of sorcery, he was in front of the barber shop . . .

He got off the horse faster than he intended, but managed somehow to stay on his feet. The horse stood patiently as he clung with his left hand to the saddle horn and waited for the town to cease spinning about him like a whirligig. And then he was ready. With an unsteady hand he tied the horse's reins to the hitch rail. And then he started up the long wooden flight of steps that led to the doctor's office. A dim light showed in a back window.

Halfway up he found himself slumped against the railing, sucking in huge gulps of air, sweat standing out on his face and neck and crawling down the middle of his back. From that point on he used his left hand to pull himself up the steps. On the landing, he leaned against the doorjamb and knocked.

He was ready to collapse and he knew it. But he couldn't quit now. He knocked a second time and tried to make it louder than the first.

The door swung open and Kyle lurched into the dim room. He felt strong, wiry hands supporting him, guiding him swiftly into a further room. And then he was falling onto something soft that squeaked and caught him and carried him into nothingness . . .

# 6

Clay Allison grunted in dismay, looked around the table at the other players, then forced a smile. He had discarded a deuce, a six of clubs, and a four of spades. What he had gotten back was two threes and a six of hearts — to go with two jacks. Two pair, jack high. It wasn't worth betting on, and he knew it.

He knew it because of the way the cards had been running all morning. He knew it because of the chill he felt in his bones — a chill that had been building all this week, from everyone in Cody. This sort of thing had happened before to Clay Allison — whenever he had run out his string in a town. Or a territory. He slammed down his cards and got up.

"I'm cashing in my chips," he told the men at the table as he gathered in the two small stacks still left by his place. He did not like way that sounded, but the words were out before he had known what he was going to say.

The men at the table exchanged glances and one of them — a hardware clerk — smirked momentarily. Clay felt like wiping out that grin with the barrel of his Colt. Instead he straightened his shoulders and carried his chips over to the bar.

With what little he had left, he bought himself a beer and swilled it down gloomily. The barkeep sensed his mood and stayed at the far end of the bar after serving him, busying himself with polishing glasses. The sound of the horses clopping by on the hard-packed street outside the hotel saloon increased his restlessness. At last, he slammed the empty stein down upon the bar and strode belligerently through the small lobby of the hotel and out onto the porch.

Sick of sitting, he leaned on one of the porch pillars and took out his last cheroot and lit up. Sucking the smoke into his lungs gave him no comfort at all, however. It was almost a week now since he had arrived back in Cody on the lookout for Kyle Robinson — but the man had not showed. Clay had ridden out to Kyle's valley spread twice during the week in hopes of picking up sign. He had found the spot where the J Bar cattle Kyle had found had scattered. Some were still nosing around the blackened ruins of the place. And he had caught the tracks of his two partners as they charged out from behind the barn, galloped across the stream and then lit out for the pass. But the cattle's hoofprints had made it impossible to find any clear sign of Robinson's horse — if he were still on a horse.

Of course there was always the possibility that Robinson was dead somewhere. Warner had said distinctly that they had winged him. But without a body, Clay could not take anything for granted. And if Robinson was alive and made it back here to Cody, there was a good chance he would be able to identify Rick and Frenchie as the ones who had burned him out and attempted to bushwhack him.

And that would put Clay — and

Beecher — on the spot.

Clay's plan had been to bring in the body of Kyle Robinson — and with it the bodies of Rick Warner and Frenchie, explaining that they had gotten out of hand and that when he had caught them burning out Robinson's place, he had been forced to go after them. Robinson had joined him in the effort, and had stopped a bullet. There would have been hell to pay and head-shakin' aplenty at such a story, but it would be his word and they would all be stuck with it. After a while, the talk would have died down. Memories were short in a cattle town — and then Clay would have been able to move in on Beecher and that girl of his . . .

The thought of Joanne Beecher caused Clay to shift his position and lean away from the porch post. Once he had allowed himself to think of her as a possibility, something hard and remote within him had softened and left him oddly vulnerable. And unable to prevent his thoughts from dwelling on her constantly. It was like an obsession. He knew it and hated it, but found there was little he could do to curb his restless hunger for her.

He shook his head at the irony of it, then leaned back against the post and chided himself. What was the matter with him? He was close to panic. He was thinking it was all over, that he had no chance with her when there was a good likelihood he had played his cards to perfection and was indeed on the threshold of success. *Kyle Robinson is dead!* he told himself with sudden vehemence. *He's lyin' out there, rottin' to death somewhere in the mountains! Send Frenchie and Warner south. Give them what you promised and get rid of them!*

It was startling how simple this solution was. It was Warner and Frenchie that Joanne could not abide. They were always snickering and sending foul glances in her direction. Their lust for her stank like a buffalo hunter's blanket. It even made him uncomfortable.

But with them gone. And the canyon ranch shut down. He would have a chance with her. Yes, he would.

He felt better at once and straightened,

intending to go for his horse and ride out to the canyon ranch. But as he started down the hotel-porch steps, she came riding in from the east — so suddenly that it caused his pulse to lift. It was almost as if his thinking of her had had the power to create her out of thin air.

He paused on the wooden walk in front of the hotel and watched her ride in. She caught sight of him as she drew abreast of the hotel, and drew in the broad-chested blue she was riding. She was dressed in her black wide-brimmed hat, silk blouse under a black vest, and a dark woolen split skirt. Her long chestnut hair she had tied back into a bun.

As she acknowledged his polite greeting with a curt nod, her dark eyes snapped with sullen displeasure.

"I haven't seen you since the funeral, Sheriff," she said. "Nor your two sidekicks for a longer time. I was hoping you were gone too."

He swallowed his sudden anger and felt his face darkening. At the same time he was aware of how he must look to this cool witch of a woman: shaggy white hair, untrimmed, yellowed mustache, and a belly beginning to sag uncomfortably around his cartridge belt. "I'm still here, Miss Beecher. No need for me to go anywhere. Leastways, not while I'm still the sheriff of Cody County."

"I was hoping my father had taken my advice and sent you off."

"He didn't, Miss Beecher. It's the voters have to do that."

"Nonsense. You'd go if he told you to go."

By this time the chill he had felt earlier during the card game returned to Clay. He caught the eyes of the crowd that had gathered and the look of furtive satisfaction on so many of the faces. Just as she was supposed to have whipsawed Tim Landon in front of the townspeople, she was giving it to him. By Judas Priest! Someday soon he'd take this filly down a peg!

"Well, I ain't goin' nowhere, Miss Beecher," he told her with sullen force.

"I suppose I've made it impossible for you to leave gracefully now, haven't I." She shook her head in disgust at herself.

"For that, I am sorry. Good afternoon, Sheriff."

She started up again and he watched her ride as far as the barber's and pull into the hitch rail. She was going up to see that lawyer, he realized. He looked quickly around him at the crowd that had not yet completely dispersed, hoping to find a grin or a careless remark — any excuse to lash out.

But no one met his eye, and all he saw were furtive backs as the townspeople rushed off to discuss with bright eyes and twisted mouths the hard words that had flown between Joanne Beecher and Clay Allison.

Clay turned and shouldered his way back into the hotel saloon, intent on a whiskey and possibly a face to push in, all thought of riding out to the canyon ranch wiped completely from his mind.

\*    \*    \*

Kyle put the glass of water down and leaned close to hear what Tim said.

"Thanks," the man whispered. He did

not open his eyes as he spoke, and once he had thanked Kyle he slowly turned his head to the wall. Kyle watched the man a moment longer, took a deep breath and stood up. He was in the long anteroom beyond Doc Fletcher's consulting room. A sling hung loosely around his neck, since he only rested his right arm in it occasionally now and was intent on going without it entirely. He had deliberately held the glass for Tim with his right hand.

Doc Fletcher was standing in the doorway, a cup of whiskey in his hand. He had been watching as Kyle gave Tim the sip of water.

"Well, that's some improvement anyway," the doctor said, his long, saturnine face smiling faintly. "At least now he can tell us when he's thirsty."

"You think he'll be all right?"

"Head injuries are always tough ones to call, Kyle," the doctor replied. "But that flap of bone that was impinging on the meningeal sac has been taken care of. So we'll see."

Kyle looked back down at the lawyer. Kyle had held the lamp the night Doc

Fletcher drilled into Landon's skull and bent the bone back into place. At the moment Tim's entire head was swathed in bandages, and it was a fact that only after the operation did Tim begin to come around.

"The only question," said the doctor, lifting the cup of whiskey to his lips, "is whether or not he'll have all his faculties when he does come around. There might have been considerable brain damage."

"Like what?"

"Ever see anyone who was kicked by a mule?"

"No. But I remember a fellow on the ranch in Texas where I grew up. His father was a blacksmith and he had been helping one day. A horse kicked him. He was never much good after that. Funny thing. He loved birds. Said he could hear them — even when they weren't singing." Kyle shook his head and looked back down at Tim. "None of us laughed. He grew into a strapping fellow, as big as his old man — but with the understanding of a child."

"Well," Doc Fletcher said, looking shrewdly into the empty cup in his hand. "That's what I meant."

As the doctor turned to go back into his office, there was a rap on the outer door and then it was pushed open. Looking beyond the doctor, Kyle saw Joanne Beecher step into the outer office.

Their eyes met. He saw the astonishment on her face. And the fear as well.

Curious, Kyle followed the doctor through his consulting room and stood beside him as he greeted the rancher's daughter.

"What brings you here, Joanne?" the doctor asked. "You don't look sick at all — the very picture of health, in fact."

She looked nervously from the doctor to Kyle, then back to the doctor. "I came to see . . . about Tim. I was wondering how he was."

"A little better," the doctor said. "As a matter of fact, he just spoke out and asked Kyle here for a glass of water. We are both encouraged by this response to the operation."

"Operation?" She seemed appalled.

The tall man bent his head in acknowledgment of her concern. "Yes, indeed. An operation. Seems your friends managed to crack Tim's skull well enough to cause great internal pressure and bleeding."

Her face had paled at the doctor's ruthless account of Tim's injury, and for a moment Kyle was a little sorry for her. But she recovered nicely.

"Well, then. I am sure he'll be all right now." She held her head back slightly, proudly. "Won't he?"

The doctor shrugged. "We'll see."

"You mean you're not sure?"

The doctor turned his back on the girl and walked through the open doorway to his desk, on top of which the bottle of whiskey was waiting. As he unstoppered it and poured a healthy dollop into the white cup, he glanced at Kyle.

"Why don't you tell her," he said wearily.

Kyle explained quickly to Joanne about the possibility of brain damage. When he had finished, the girl seemed considerably subdued. Without a word she moved back to one of the wooden chairs against the wall and sat down.

"I *am* sorry," she said in a small voice. "If my words had anything to do with this . . ." She glanced into the room where Tim lay, and then suddenly dropped her face into her hands and began to cry softly.

Kyle started toward her, but the doctor waved him off with a shake of his head and then brought his cup of whiskey over to her and held it in front of her face.

"Take a sip of medicine, Joanne," he said. "The best kind."

She looked up at him, the tears streaming down her face. With the back of one hand she wiped both cheeks, with the other she took the cup and, giving the doctor a grateful smile, took a healthy belt of the doc's prescription.

"Feel better?"

She compressed her lips and nodded bravely.

"Good. Then I have some more bad news for you."

She frowned.

"You got any idea what Kyle Robinson

is doing in here with me?"

She shook her head, then glanced over at him. "I thought you might have left the county."

"He might as well. He's been burned out by your boys."

"Burned out?"

Kyle spoke up then. "Rick Warner and Frenchie burned down my cabin and the barn. They also tried to kill me."

Joanne looked to the doctor for confirmation. She obviously did not want to believe what Kyle was telling her. The doctor nodded.

"He fell into my office in the middle of the night last Friday with a slug in his shoulder. I took it out for him and cauterized the wound with good medicine, the best — and he's doing fine now. But he hasn't got much of a spread with both his cabin and barn gone."

"I swear, Doc," she said softly, "I knew nothing of this. Nothing."

"And your father?"

She started to deny that he could have had anything to do with it, and then caught herself. It was obvious to Kyle that at that moment she wasn't sure if her father had been a party to what had happened to him or not. But the thought that he might have instigated the action by Warner and Frenchie genuinely appalled her. She looked directly at Kyle, then got to her feet. "I don't know if he did or not, Mr. Robinson," she told him. "I relayed your threat to him. You remember. We were *all* going to pay for our part in Ramirez's death."

"Jose Ramirez and his wife. Yes, I remember."

"So, perhaps . . ." She shrugged despairingly.

She looked around at the doctor. "Where does all this end, Doctor Fletcher?"

"That's a good question, Joanne. Now you see why we have courts — and lawyers."

She flinched at that and looked beyond him in at Tim Landon. "May I see him?" she asked.

With a shrug, the doctor stood aside to let her enter his consulting room. She walked through it as the two men watched her without following. She paused beside Tim's cot, then bent and called his name softly. But there was obviously no response. She straightened unhappily and returned to the doctor and Kyle.

"He didn't seem to notice me," she said.

"He needs the rest," the doctor said kindly. "He was probably asleep."

"No. He turned and looked at me. But it was like he didn't see me. Like he was looking through me."

"He's tired."

"Yes. Of course."

Her face became cold. She looked at Kyle.

"What part do you think Sheriff Clay Allison might have had in burning you out, Mr. Robinson?"

"Those two were friends of his, weren't they?"

"They came up with him from Texas."

"Well, I didn't see the sheriff, Miss Beecher, but I sure as hell saw his two sidekicks."

"Of course he's involved," she said. She took a deep breath. "I am going back to the Double B. Perhaps now my father will listen to me and get rid of that awful man — and his Texas gang."

"I can take care of them, Miss Beecher."

"I am sure you can, Mr. Robinson. I just don't want them on Double B's payroll when you do — or when you make good on that promise of yours, and come after my father and me."

Before Kyle could reply, she had brushed past him, swept up her wide-brimmed hat from the chair and disappeared out the door. In the sudden silence they could hear her heels on the outside steps as she descended to the street. The doctor looked at Kyle, a faint smile on his long face.

"That's a lot of woman, Kyle. Tough. Wrongheaded maybe. But when she comes and when she goes, you know she's been by."

Kyle nodded. "I reckon you do, at that."

The doctor went back to his desk and pulled open the large bottom drawer on the right. It contained Kyle's holstered

Colt and gunbelt. Pulling it out and dropping it onto the desk, he looked at Kyle.

"I guess you're fit enough by now."

"That's what I was thinking, all right. Where's my hat?"

As Kyle buckled on his six-gun, the doctor pulled his hat down out of a shelf over the medicine cabinet. Kyle was standing in a faded-blue cotton shirt and faded Levi's, freshly laundered by the doctor's laundress while Kyle was on his back. His horse, saddle and gear had been left with the hostler at the livery, the doctor having impressed on the man the necessity for keeping his mouth shut about the horse's owner.

Kyle pulled his hat down securely and smiled gratefully at the doctor. "I owe you a lot, Doc."

"Hell, I know that. Just wait'll you get my bill. Now go on out of here and don't let the light of day blind you."

Kyle nodded, dropped his sling onto a chair and pulled open the door and stepped out onto the landing. The sun was still high above the town and the world had never appeared so bright and clean to him. He'd been holed up in the doctor's office for close to a week and this sudden emergence into the world of the living caused him to realize once again how lucky he had been in surviving all that he had to reach this moment in his life. But the doctor was right: the sunlight was dazzling — magnificent, but dazzling.

He turned and looked at the doctor. "Thanks, Doc. See you around."

"I hope." The man closed the door.

Kyle kept hold of the railing as he descended the steps, remembering vividly now his condition when he had come up them a week before with the moon as his sun. Now his shoulder was just a mite stiff, his arm a bit weak. And he had been working to strengthen his right hand. Fletcher had given him a rubber ball to squeeze and he had squeezed it continuously. Even as he recalled this and reached the wooden walk at the foot of the steps, he began flexing his right hand.

If Warner or Frenchie appeared, he needed to be ready.

Joanne was well out of town by this time. He could see her in the distance astride a large blue. She rode well, sitting her mount straight and tall, he noted. And then she was gone from his sight as the cloud of dust her mount raised drifted between her and the town.

Coming to a halt then, he found himself standing in front of the street entrance to the hotel saloon. For the first time he realised what a gargantuan thirst he had acquired during the past week — not for that medicine the doctor favored, but for a tall cool glass of beer. He shouldered his way through the batwings, walked across the sawdust-covered floor and bellied up to the bar.

"Beer," he told the tall, balding barkeep.

The man seemed unduly nervous as he poured. Kyle gave it no heed as he paid him and pulled the stein toward him. He took a generous swallow, wiped the suds from his mouth, turned around and glanced idly about the room — the same room, he realized grimly, where Tim Landon had been beaten so unmercifully.

Sheriff Clay Allison was sitting at a table in the far corner with three others. Playing poker, they were — only Allison seemed to be having some difficulty playing at the moment. His companions in the game were busy glancing in Kyle's direction, and Allison was watching Kyle furtively from under the brim of his hat. The game's progress had all but frozen as each man at the table watched for Kyle's next move.

Kyle drank his beer, slowly. The sight of Clay Allison was filling him with a smoky fury. He needed the beer to calm himself, using the time it gave him to bank the fire that smoldered in his gut. But he could not deny the reckless exhilaration he felt at finding the man so near at hand. He continued to sip his beer.

Abruptly he shifted the beer to his left hand and let his right hand drop to his side. He flexed his fingers quickly. They were working just fine.

He finished his beer. Without looking back, he placed the empty stein down on the bar surface and then pushed himself away from the bar. Clay Allison sprang to his feet, his chair tumbling backward to the floor. The other players scrambled from the table and were out of Kyle's line of sight in a matter of seconds.

Kyle forced himself to pull up and smile at Allison. He had no desire — he suddenly reminded himself — to draw on Allison in this place. He would get the man eventually. Of that, he had no doubt. But Kyle wanted the others as well. "No need to go for your gun, Allison," Kyle said. "Just tell me where Warner and Frenchie are holed up."

Clay's eyes narrowed. "What do you want them for?"

"They burnt me out — then tried to bushwhack me. I figure you or Beecher put them up to it. Right?"

"You're crazy, Robinson. I had nothing to do with that."

"Just tell me where they are, Allison."

"You won't find them," the sheriff said. "They're probably halfway to Texas by now." He smiled. "They left last week."

"Both of them?"

Allison hesitated only a second, but Kyle caught it. "Sure. Both of them."

"Frenchie, too? He rode out last week?"

"You heard me."

"You're a liar, Allison. I caught Frenchie in the back with a slug. It was a solid hit, not a flesh wound. He had considerable trouble staying on his horse. If he's halfway to Texas, someone's carrying him there in a pine box."

"Hell, Robinson. You asked me where they were and I told you. If you don't want to believe me, that's your problem."

Kyle looked at the sheriff. Allison had already told Kyle more than he realized. If he had lied about Frenchie's condition, he was probably lying all the way. The two men were still in the area, then. Frenchie, at least. And perhaps Warner.

"Sit down, Sheriff," Kyle said, "and finish your poker game. Just don't try to bluff, that's all. You ain't worth a damn at it."

Allison started to turn back to the table to do just as Kyle suggested until he caught himself, his face darkening, and strode angrily past Kyle and out of the saloon. Kyle followed after him and watched the sheriff until he turned at last into the office he had been provided in Cody's small jailhouse.

Kyle turned back into the saloon for another beer. If any of the sheriff's champions in the place wanted to stand up for the man, Kyle would be glad to oblige. But no one bothered him as he bought his second beer and brought it to a corner table.

He was drinking it sometime later when Doc Fletcher entered, looked quickly around, then started at once for Kyle's table. The fact that the doctor did not stop at the bar first alerted Kyle. At once he thought of Tim Landon and started to get up.

"Sit down," the doctor said, slipping into a chair across the table from Kyle. "You're right. It's Tim. But there's nothing you — or anyone else — can do for him now. The blacksmith lugged him down from my office and is working on the coffin right now behind the barber shop." He shook his head wearily. "I

142

hated to lose that man, Kyle. And I try to tell myself that it's for the best. Most likely, if Tim had pulled through, he'd have been little more than a vegetable."

Kyle didn't know what to say. The doctor's face looked surprisingly drawn, the eyes bleak and empty. He had thought of the man as a sardonic, distant observer of men's follies, well enough detached not to be let a single man's death affect him this strongly. But he had been wrong. Kyle saw now that each man he lost, each instance of a futile and senseless death left the doctor a little more ragged, a step closer to despair. No wonder he drank so heavily. And no wonder it was so difficult for the man to get himself drunk.

Kyle stared down at his half-full stein of beer. "I never got to know him, Doc. But what little I saw of him made me like him. Just one thing puzzles me. How come Tim Landon was so sure Jose didn't kill Jed Beecher?"

"I guess that was my fault, Kyle."

"*Your* fault?"

"I'm what passes for the county

coroner in these parts, and when Burnside was fitting Jed for his coffin, he discovered something and called me down."

"What was it?"

The doctor spoke carefully and kept his voice low. "Jed had taken a long fall off someplace pretty high and landed in water. Both legs and at least four ribs were broken. In addition, his lungs had water in them. Burnside discovered that when he rolled Jed over."

Kyle frowned. "Go on."

"Jed was not killed where he was found, Kyle. He was killed someplace else, then dumped on Jose's land — an obvious attempt to frame Jose."

"And Tim found this out?"

"I told him. That's why he refused to prosecute Jose — and why Prescott backed him up. Besides that, I always had the feeling that Tim and Jose were on to something — about the rustling that was hurting Beecher so much."

"What?"

"I never found out — and after Jed's death, everything was so wild, I lost track of things. Now Tim's dead — and I sure as hell don't like to think what we've traded him for."

"Me neither, Doc."

The doctor fixed Kyle with a hard gaze. "You mean that, Kyle?"

"I mean it."

"Judge Prescott wants me to bring you over to his chambers, Kyle. I just got through speaking to him. I went over to see him after Tim died."

"Prescott? What's he want with me?"

The doctor smiled bleakly. "Why don't you let him tell you, Kyle?"

Kyle looked into the doctor's haunted eyes for a full moment, then shrugged his shoulders. "Sure, Doc. Be right with you." Kyle finished his glass of beer, wiped his mouth off with the back of his hand, then got decisively to his feet.

The doctor led the way out of the saloon.

The judge held court in the hardware store when it was needed. His office was on the second floor, just above the store. Kyle and Doctor Fletcher were halfway across the street when Kyle heard the sudden, ominous clatter of hoofs.

He glanced to his right just in time to see Clay Allison, aboard a powerful bay and bearing down on them both. He was using his quirt on the animal and roweling it furiously as he kept the horse on a steady course directly for them. Kyle heard a warning shout from the board walk behind him as he reached out and flung the doctor violently to one side, then dove after the man.

The ground shook under him and he felt a hoof brush the back of his vest while the long shadow of the powerful animal passed over his prostrate form. Dust enveloped him as the sound of hoofs began to recede. Kyle scrambled to his feet, drawing and cocking his Colt as he did so. But he had to hold up his left arm to ward off the clouds of choking dust that settled upon him. When he realized he would have no chance of bringing down the sheriff, he holstered his gun and turned to see about the doctor.

He was sitting up in the dust dazedly as townsmen rushed out into the street toward him. He grinned sardonically up at Kyle as Kyle reached down and hauled him to his feet. The two men paused then to brush themselves off. As Kyle pushed through the excited townsmen and headed for the board walk, he saw Judge Prescott standing in front of the hardware store.

Still brushing himself off, he stepped up onto the walk and addressed the judge: "Just what was it you had in mind, Judge?"

"Step inside, Mr. Robinson. Seems to me you'll be mighty interested in my proposition." He looked carefully at the doctor. "You all right, Sam?"

"I'm still swallowing dust," the doctor replied. "But I'm all right. Thanks to Kyle here."

The judge's office was lined with books, thick, heavy ones that seemed surprisingly well worn. Two extraordinarily large volumes were open on the judge's desk, which was litter of documents and writing utensils. The smell of ink hung heavy in the room.

The judge moved around his desk, sat in his large swivel chair and pawed among the papers scattered over the green blotter, fished out a telegram and handed it up to Kyle. Kyle took it, read it, then looked back at the judge.

"It says you've got the power to appoint a deputy U.S. marshal."

"And it's signed by the territorial governor, Kyle."

Kyle looked at the doctor, then back at the judge. "What's this got to do with me?"

"You mean you haven't figured that out yet?"

Kyle dropped the telegram back onto the judge's desk. "Sure I have. But I'm not a lawman."

"No, you're not. But I'm thinking you'd make a good one — with plenty of incentive." He pulled open a drawer, picked up a badge sitting in it and handed it up to Kyle. "Here. Pin it on, Kyle. You're Cody's new Deputy U.S. Marshal."

Kyle did not take the badge. "I'm not your man, Judge. A peace officer I am not. You ought to look into a man's background before you offer him a badge. I've raised hell from here to Texas."

"So you have. I have no doubt of that, Kyle. But that's not the point. I think you can bring in the man that murdered Tim Landon. And you're the only man in sight who can do that chore for me. We sure as hell can't count on Sheriff Clay Allison."

Kyle shifted his feet and shot a glance at the doctor. He found no help from that quarter and looked back at the judge. Of course the man was right. Clay Allison had gone rogue, and even if he hadn't, there would have been little likelihood that he could have been induced to go after Borrmann for the killing of Landon. Hell, in a sense he had participated in it.

And there was the fact of his earlier . . .

Kyle held out his hand for the badge.

"Fine," said the judge. "We'll get the town council together and swear you in this afternoon."

Kyle fingered the badge, then looked at the judge. "There's just one thing, Judge. I'd like more than one warrant. I'd like two more — for Rick Warner and Frenchie Wells."

The judge glanced at the doctor, then back at Kyle. "For burning out your place?"

"And for trying to bushwhack me."

"It'll be your word against theirs."

"I know that."

The judge's eyes narrowed. "This has nothing to do with . . . that other business."

"Of course not, Judge," Kyle replied, his voice flat.

The judge accepted Kyle's denial at face value, even though both men knew otherwise, and nodded. "The three warrants will be ready this afternoon at the swearing in, Kyle."

"Thank you, Judge."

## 7

Carl Beecher spun angrily to face his daughter.

"Well, what did you expect?" he demanded. "He threatened all of us. He's killed two of my hands! Of course I sent Allison over there to burn him out."

"And to bushwhack him."

"No. That was not part of it, Joanne. Believe me."

Joanne slumped back onto the horsehair sofa. She felt suddenly drained. The sight of her father turning on her like an animal at bay saddened her. He was standing now behind his swivel chair, his back to the window, pain and frustration etched starkly on his weatherbeaten face. Not until this moment had she realized what all this had done to her father. In these few terrible weeks since Jed's death, he'd been reduced to an old man. An indomitable, fierce old man, to be sure. But an old man, nevertheless.

And during all this time the only thing she had considered was her own grief.

She looked away from her father, and shuddered. She felt cold all of a sudden. "It's all right, Father," she said. "I have no right complaining. Of course Robinson is dangerous. And I can see how you must have felt with him coming in and taking over where that Mex had left off — the same thing all over again. And maybe you didn't tell Warner or Frenchie to kill him, but I can see where they wouldn't even figure they had to ask. Of course we would want Kyle Robinson killed." She looked up at her father then. "He's standing in Double B's way."

Her father flinched. Then moving around his chair, he slumped into it and leaned his elbows wearily on the desk, his eyes on his daughter. "Don't you see, Joanne? This is the only option a man has if he wants to hold on to what he's built up. We're just like cattle after a long winter with the wolves circling and getting closer if we don't fight back. Any way we know how."

"*Any* way?"

"Yes, damn it! Any way."

"So we import killers like Clay Allison and his bunch from Texas. That's what we have to do to hold on to Double B."

"Yes." But he spoke without his usual authority, with a weariness that seemed to have drained him, utterly and completely. "Yes, Joanne," he repeated. "That's what we have to do."

"I'm sorry for us, Father," she heard herself say, her voice betraying the desperation she felt. She got to her feet and looked at her father without rancor, sorry now that she had lashed out at him with such fury earlier. "Jed is dead. Tim Landon is dying. And it's not over yet. For either of us."

She turned and hurried from the room.

Outside, she drank in the cool, clear sunlight and felt enormous relief to be out of the main house and away from the conflict with her father. She had ridden in angrily not long before, but now she felt a need to saddle up again and ride out, this time ranging over Double B's holdings. She was anxious suddenly to see once again the intoxicating sweep of their grasslands, to let the sharp scent of sage cloud her senses as she rode, to feel under her the soft thud of hoofs on thick, luxuriant turf. What she needed was tangible proof that this land she loved was still there and worth the blood and heartache it was costing them.

She called across the yard to the horse wrangler Andy and told him to saddle up her blue again. Then she strode swiftly across the yard toward the stable, waving to Callahan the blacksmith as she went. He was watching her from the doorway of his shed, his enormous hammer clutched in one brawny fist.

The sound of an approaching horseman alerted her. She turned, squinted into the sunlight and caught sight of Clay Allison nearing the outer gate. Eager to have as little to do with the man as possible, she hurried into the cool stable where Andy was saddling the blue.

Beecher was standing in the open door of the ranchhouse when Clay dismounted and mounted the low front porch.

"I saw you from the window," Beecher told him.

Clay nodded, swept off his hat and mopped his brow with his bandanna.

"Well, what is it?"

"You gonna make me stand out here, Carl?"

Beecher turned in the doorway and led the way into the house. "Come inside, then."

Clay kept his temper and followed the big man as he led him into his study. The leather couch along the wall looked comfortable, and after the ride he had just completed he moved toward it quickly. Before it could accept his weary body, however, Beecher was questioning him again.

"Why are you here, Clay?"

Dropping wearily onto the couch, Allison fixed the older man with a sardonic gaze. "I got news, Carl."

"Bad news, I take it."

"I got word — just before I lit out — that Kyle Robinson's going to get a deputy U.S. marshal's badge. Judge Prescott's got the authorization from the Governor. The telegram came this morning."

"You sure of this?"

"When I rode out I saw Robinson and the Doc on their way over to the judge's office. Leastways, that's the way it looked to me."

Beecher had been standing beside his desk when Allison entered. Now he moved around behind it, slumped down into his high-backed leather chair and leaned back, contemplating the sheriff balefully.

"And that ain't all," Clay continued.

Beecher closed his eyes for a moment, then nodded imperceptibly to the sheriff. "Let's have it, Allison."

"Tim Landon is dead."

Beecher said nothing for a long while. Clay waited for the man's response. His face had lost its color for a few seconds. When it returned, Beecher said, "I didn't want that, Clay. You know I didn't.

Though Landon had become our enemy, his death was something neither Joanne nor I wanted."

"It wasn't me did it, Carl. It was Borrmann."

The big man shook his head decisively. "As I told you before, Clay. You should have stopped Borrmann. Instead, you even let Rick put in his two cents."

"You said it yourself. Tim Landon was an enemy to Double B."

"And dead, he's a finger pointing at the Double B — an accusing finger, Clay. It says that we kill our enemies, even when they work within the law. The death of that Mex was something else again. I'll even stand still for the death of his squaw. But not Tim Landon. I can't abide that, Clay. Joanne wouldn't let me. And no one in Cody will either."

Clay nodded. He had expected the old man to unwind when he heard of Landon's death. But there was more, and he hesitated to tell the man.

But Beecher caught the hesitation — and its significance. "Let's have it, Clay. All of it."

"We burned out Kyle Robinson, like you told us, but — "

". . . when your boys tried to kill him, he got away."

Clay frowned. "You knew?"

"Joanne told me. She just left this room, Clay — a most unhappy woman. I had to explain to her that bushwhacking Robinson was not my idea. I hope she believed me."

"I don't know what got into those two, Carl. I told them I just wanted that Mex's place burnt out. I didn't say anything at all about Robinson." Allison looked shrewdly at Beecher. "Of course, it might be he just came upon them while they was setting the torch to his buildings and just naturally started throwing lead."

"It doesn't matter, Clay," Beecher said softly. "It's all over now. The Mex is gone. And we've cleaned the range of any nester or rancher that threatened to hem us in. But after Tim Landon's death and the botched attempt to bushwhack Robinson, I figure we don't need your services any longer."

"That's Joanne talking, Carl."

"Maybe it is. But she's a smart girl, Clay — and for the last week or so she's been talking good sense."

"That's not the way she sounded when she wanted us to throw down on that Mex."

"I know that, Clay. But I'm grateful for the change. It wasn't seemly for her to lust after a man's death like that. Even if the man was a Mex."

"So now you just toss me and my boys aside like we was empty jugs. Is that it, Carl?"

"I sent for you to do a job, Clay. The job is done. Why not look at it that way?"

"The job ain't done. Kyle Robinson's got a badge on his vest and he's going to be a real burr under your saddle, Carl."

"Not if you and your boys — and that includes Borrmann — get on your horses and make tracks. And I expect you to do just that."

Clay Allison stood up. He was furious, but he was hiding his feelings as well as he knew how. This was not the way he had wanted things to go. After all, with Jed gone and Kyle Robinson on the prod,

Clay had seen himself as the rancher's only recourse. The thought had filled him with elation as he rode the long miles out to the Double B this day.

He had even gotten himself to thinking maybe Joanne Beecher could be brought around, once she got used to him ramrodding Double B punchers and cattle. He had planned on burning the canyon ranch and sending Rick and the others south.

But it had not been part of his plan to go himself.

"All right, Carl," Allison said. "It's over. We done our job, the one you called us up here to do. But that don't mean I have to go, does it? Hell, I'm still the sheriff of Cody County."

"You go too, Clay. You can leave your sheriff's badge with me. I will accept your resignation."

"Not if I don't give it to you."

The man sighed. "Are you thinking of turning on me, Clay? After all these years? I can buy and sell you, mister. I'm tired, but not too tired to tangle with you. I want you to take your boys and go back to Texas. Is that clear?''

Allison took in a deep lungful of air. Then he nodded.

''But I'm not an unfair man, Clay. Not to those who serve me faithfully. And that, I must admit, you have done. You will not be returning to Texas empty-handed.''

Clay waited, greed stirring like a spring seedling within him, as Beecher got up and walked over to the huge safe in the corner. It was not locked and Beecher yanked the handle down and pulled open the heavy door. From where he was standing, Clay saw the bulging sacks of silver on the first and second shelves. Neat stacks of bills filled most of the other shelves, with an untidy profusion of ledgers on the bottom shelf.

Beecher took out one stack of bills, closed the safe's door, and returned to the desk. Slipping off the elastic band from around the money, he began counting quietly. When he finished, he gathered up the bills he had dropped onto his desk and handed them across to Clay.

As Clay took the money, Beecher said, ''I think you'll agree, Clay, that I've been more than generous. There's a thousand dollars there for each of your boys, two thousand for you — and I've even included five hundred for Borrmann. He is a stupid man and I don't feel that I owe him a thing. But I want to be fair."

Clay counted the bills quickly. Beecher was being very fair to him, Clay realized. But Clay could not keep out of his mind the glimpse he had just been given of the contents of Beecher's safe. The payoff to Borrmann and his men was generous, of course, yet it was only a tiny fraction of what the man could afford. Clay had himself been putting a bit aside these past months and was not suffering as a result. Indeed, his saddlebags were packed tightly with loot. Still, like this payoff, it was a paltry sum when compared with the riches this old Croesus had amassed.

"Thanks, Carl," Allison told Beecher. "I'm sure the boys will be satisfied."

"And you?"

Clay shrugged. "I wanted to stay, Carl. You know that."

"I'm sorry, Clay. But my decision is final."

"Yeah. I guess it is, at that." Allison folded the bills and stuffed them into the hip pocket of his jeans, then reached back to the sofa for his hat and slapped it on. He looked coldly at his former partner. "If this Kyle Robinson ties a can to your tail, Carl, don't come runnin' to me. I'll be where the sun is warm and the grass tall. And that's where I aim to stay."

Beecher nodded shortly. "Fair enough, Clay."

Clay touched his hat brim in salute, turned and strode from the room.

*  *  *

Something within her, an uneasiness she could not dispel had drawn Joanne to this high valley. She told herself she was curious to see just how badly damaged the J Bar Ranch buildings were. And in the back of her mind there was the nagging hope that it was not as bad as she had been led to believe by the doctor and Kyle Robinson. But it was the uneasiness more than anything else that had prompted her to guide her mount onto Robinson's land.

And that uneasiness was the result of her wide-ranging sweep over Double B's lush grasslands — a lushness that encouraged her on the one hand and troubled her deeply on the other. *Where were all the Double B stock she had seen but a few weeks earlier?*

The Mex had been scrambling for his scalp for better than a month before his death, and Kyle Robinson had not yet had a chance to establish himself. Indeed, he had spent the last week holed up in the doc's office. Neither the Mex nor Robinson had been in any position to rustle Double B stock during these past weeks. So where was it? Why was Double B still losing cattle? The question sickened her. After all they had done — to themselves and to others — why was the Double B still so pathetically vulnerable? She was close to despair as she rode, searching the grasslands that opened out before her, anxious to find some sign of their beef that might have followed the creek up into this valley.

As the valley walls — faced with giant white outcroppings of rock and tenacious patches of gnarled juniper — closed in on her, she guided the blue along the spine of a ridge that paralleled the creek, lifting her eventually so that she could see far up the valley — even to the tangled, charred remains of the J Bar. Her heart sank within her as she rode closer to the burnt-out ranch. There was nothing so heart-wringing, she felt, as the sight of what was once someone's home burnt to the ground.

She was close enough to see the individual blackened timbers of the barn when she pulled up abruptly, bringing the big blue to a snorting halt. She hastily patted its neck, sorry for the whipping her sudden tug on the reins had given the blue's mouth. But even as she comforted the horse, she was listening intently. Far below the ridge, out of sight in a clump of cottonwoods and willows, men were driving cattle. She could hear the distant bawling of the animals and the occasional whistles of the drovers as they pushed the beef along.

Joanne guided her mount into a clump of pine and sat quietly to wait for the men and the cattle to emerge from the trees. The beef came first, spilling out across the flat just below the burnt-out ranch. Then came the cowboys. There were two of them — and she recognized them at once.

Smoke Wilson and Toby Baxter.

They were two of her father's most trusted hands. When many of their hands had left because her father had imported the four Texans, Smoke and Toby had remained loyal and stayed on. At Jed's death, Smoke had been appointed temporary ramrod until her father could find a younger and a tougher man. Joanne had every reason to trust these two men, having known them for almost as long as she could remember.

And yet, as she watched them driving the cattle before them, she felt a sharp increase in that uneasiness she had been nursing since she rode out that afternoon. Something was wrong. She could not pick out just what exactly — unless it was the way the two men were hazing the cattle. There was an urgency to it — a furtiveness, even.

They drove the cattle on past the

remains of the ranch buildings and kept on up the valley, staying close beside the creek. When they were out of sight, Joanne left the pines and allowed the blue to pick its way down the steep slope to the valley floor.

Smoke and Toby weren't taking those cattle back to the Double B. That was, by now, pretty obvious. Where, then, *were* they taking them?

Joanne meant to find out.

The trail of torn earth and fresh cow droppings was not difficult at all for Joanne to follow, and once she was at least a mile past the J Bar holdings, the trail they followed left the banks of the stream and began to climb. She found herself riding through a steep land strewn with high rocks and boulders. Occasional warped and stunted conifers found a hold between the rocks as they competed grimly for survival with a short, tough grass Joanne had not seen before. The wind became chill as Joanne climbed toward a jagged rampart of rock she had never once considered trying to breach, no matter how many times she had ridden into these mountains. She felt dwarfed and intimidated by the leaning masses of white rock that hung ominously over her, reminding her how puny a creature she was when compared with the awesome, careless shrug of these mountains.

To her right the creek slashed its way through the narrow gorge far below. Ahead of her the trail was clear — and well worn — as she noted the pulverized rock where the feet of many cattle had passed. In places where the trail narrowed and where the beef had been hazed into tight defiles, she could see the tufts of hair wedged in the rock cracks.

The sound of roaring water came to her more clearly as the blue tugged along the steep, rocky trail, lifting her well into the chill land of the snowfields. Following the trail around a massive slab of rock, she found the stream back beside the trail again, tumbling noisily through a narrow gorge. She kept going and found herself riding across a grassy shelf bordering a small, icy lake fed by a large snowfield on the far side of the shelfland.

The trail worn across this level stretch was as broad and as clearly defined as the wagon road into Cody. It led clearly around the perimeter of the lake toward a stunted clump of cedars. Beyond the trees she saw the trail — broader now — coiling out of sight below the tableland as it followed a second stream leading from the lake. As she rode across this flat, she saw the remains of many campfires along the shores of the lake and realized she had found one of the passes that led through the mountains and that it was at this point that those men driving cattle over this trail rested up, or sometimes slept through the night.

She was almost to the cedars when she noticed the sound of bawling cattle coming to her faintly across the lake, from somewhere within the gray labyrinth of rocks and narrow canyons huddled against the next great shouldering upthrust of mountains. As she rode past the stunted trees, a raw wind smelling of snow whipping at her, the click of a horse's hoof against stone brought her head around.

Smoke and Toby were riding toward her. They had been hiding in the cedars, had known she was on their trail and had simply waited for her to get past them. She had been tricked so easily, she was furious at herself.

Both men seemed uncertain and not a little sheepish as they rode up to her. Smoke was the oldest, but both men were past fifty, their sunken faces wrinkled like old leather — a gauntness about them she never seemed to have had time to notice before. Smoke's eyes were dark, somber, Toby's eyes a clear, light blue. She tried to meet both men's eyes with her own, but they would not allow it.

It was Smoke who spoke first, thumbing his hat back off his forehead. "Didn't know it was you followin' us, Miss Joanne," he said unhappily.

"What difference does that make, Smoke?"

The man shrugged his bony shoulders wearily and glanced quickly at his partner. "I guess it don't make none at that, Miss Joanne."

"Just what is this all about, Smoke?

What are you doing with Double B cattle?"

"That ain't Double B stock, Miss Joanne," Toby broke in quickly. "No, ma'am. That's J Bar cattle. We found them grazin' near the J Bar. That Robinson feller ain't been around for a week. He must a got his fill of this country and lit out. So we figgered we could sort of take it . . ."

His voice trailed off unhappily and he looked back at Smoke for help.

"Yes, Smoke," Joanne said quickly. "Where *were* you planning on taking that cattle? This is a pretty well-worn trail, I noticed. This is not the first time you men have negotiated it."

Smoke looked away from her, his right hand fiddling with his reins. Both men looked for all the world like two little boys who'd just got themselves caught raiding the cookie jar.

"Smoke, answer me. What are you men doing here? What's this all about, anyway?"

Smoke took a big breath and looked grimly at her. "I guess it ain't goin' to do us no good to lie to you, Miss Joanne."

"No, it isn't," said Joanne firmly.

Both men exchanged unhappy glances. Smoke said, "I suppose you saw all the other tracks."

"I did."

Smoke nodded. "We figured you did."

Joanne was suddenly exasperated. "Out with it, Smoke," she demanded coldly.

"I guess we been rustlin' some cattle," Smoke said. "So when we saw this J Bar stock, we just figured to rustle us some more. That's all."

*Rustlin' some cattle,* Smoke had said. The words stung her like a whip. It was a thought she had been resolutely refusing to contemplate. It couldn't be that these two ancient cowhands were behind the rustling that had all but denuded Double B ranges.

In a voice she barely recognized as her own, she said, "You mean, Smoke, that you and Toby are the ones who've been been — "

"It ain't only us," Toby broke in hastily. "We ain't the ones behind it, Miss Joanne."

Joanne turned on him. "But you know who *is* — and you've been a party to it all this time!"

The two men looked miserably at each other, then ducked their heads. Smoke and Toby had been throwing their bedrolls into the Double B chuck wagon for close on to twenty years. No one would have dared question their allegiance. Now they sat their horses before her, heads hung in mute admission of their disloyalty — their treachery. Joanne thought then of Jed's crumpled body lying face down in the grass and a terrible fury swept through her.

"You got to understand, Miss Joanne," said Toby. "We're gettin' on in years. An' we just thought we needed a nest egg. There's this little horse ranch up in Wyoming Territory, and we . . ." His voice trailed off miserably as he saw the look on Joanne's face.

"I understand perfectly, Toby," Joanne snapped coldly. "You two men are traitors to the Double B. Thieves. Men stealing from your own ranch."

The two men stared blankly at her,

offering no defense.

"Get those cattle over there," she said. "I want you to drive them back on to J Bar land — and then you're going to make a full report to my father — to the man you betrayed."

"No, we ain't," said Smoke softly, regretfully.

She watched in disbelief as the old man drew his Colt and leveled it at her. She started to demand he put away the gun. Then she saw him thumbcock the weapon and saw Toby reach back for his own gun as well.

## 8

Clay Allison had been reading sign all his life. On his way to the canyon ranch from the Double B, he had picked up Joanne's tracks. The big blue she favored left a heavy, easily recognizable hoofprint.

Following her sign into the pines atop the ridge, he had not found it difficult to read the rest of it — including who the men were who were driving the cattle. Nearly thirty head, he figured. But where the hell had those two stove-up cowpokes found this beef? And who was it told them to drive them to the canyon ranch?

Not Rick Warner. He didn't have that much initiative — not unless Frenchie was wet-nursing him. And judging from the last look he'd got at Frenchie, that man was in no kind of condition for games. He discounted Borrmann without a second thought and concluded finally that it must have been the two old coots had taken it upon themselves.

At the pass, on the small flat beside the lake, he came upon the three sets of tracks and saw at once what had happened. He spurred his mount across the flat, his fury at Beecher giving way to a delicious anticipation. He saw again in his mind's eye that safe of Beecher's, swollen with silver and currency — and knew at once that he now had the key to it.

He reached the ranch well after dark and was greeted by Borrmann standing in front of a brightly lit open doorway, a lantern held high in one hand. The sound of the rustled cattle moving restlessly in their pens back of the barn came to Allison clearly.

"That's a great target you make, Borrmann," Clay said, dismounting swiftly and handing the reins to the man. "Put the horse in the barn and get back in here. Looks like we got us some excitement. Right?"

"You know about it?"

"You mean Joanne Beecher? That's

right. I know all about it."

He left the flabbergasted Borrmann and strode into the ranchhouse, slammed the door shut behind him and found Rick Warner sitting at the table by the stove, a mug of coffee in front of him. Smoke and Toby were sitting at the table beside him. They looked very unhappy, and Clay grinned at them for a moment before looking around the big bare room.

"Where the hell is she?" he asked.

Smoke and Toby exchanged startled glances. Rick Warner grinned at Allison. "We got her tied up in the bedroom. She was shootin' off her mouth somethin' fierce, so I plugged it with a bandanna, tied her up real snug and tossed her onto the bed."

Allison nodded. "Just so's you didn't hurt her none."

"You still got an itch for that there package, Clay?"

Clay had to think on that a minute. But his answer, when it came, was certain enough. "No more. I've had my fill of the Beechers."

Allison looked at the two cowpokes

then and took a step toward the table. "What the hell got into you old coots, anyhow? Where'd you get them steers you was driving?"

"We found them around the J Bar. We figured Robinson had up and left."

"Hell. He's the new U.S. Deputy Marshal."

The two men exchanged woeful glances. Nothing they had done that day had gone right. They were in so deep now, they didn't figure they'd ever see blue sky again.

"How much did you tell her?"

"We didn't tell her nothin', Clay," piped up Toby anxiously, his gaunt face drawn with fear, his Adam's apple bouncing.

"How much does she know, then?"

"She knows enough," said Smoke unhappily. "She saw how worn that trail was. She saw the pens outside the barn. The road. She sure as hell knows now where Double B cows have been disappearin' to."

"And when she saw me," spoke up Rick, "why, she got the notion maybe you was behind this whole operation, Clay.

Don't see how she managed that." He grinned. "I tried to tell her it was all my idea."

Allison looked back at the two unhappy punchers. "I'm going to give you two some advice," Allison told them. "And you better take it. Like us, you've run out your string around these parts. Whatever gear you might have left at the Double B, go back and get it. Give Beecher your notice if you want — but then you ride, and keep right on riding. Now go out and get your mounts saddled. I'll have something for you before you ride out."

Smoke nodded. Toby swallowed hard — and nodded also. They tugged their hats down more firmly, got up from the table and brushed past Allison. As they started out the door, Borrmann hustled in with such enthusiasm he almost knocked the two punchers down. They sidestepped awkwardly and disappeared out the door.

"Where the hell they going?" Borrmann asked.

Allison didn't answer the man. He turned instead to Rick. "Where's Frenchie?"

"Hell. He died on the trail after we left you last week," Rick said, looking down into his coffee cup. "He sure as hell went fast with that slug in him."

"You bury him?"

Rick shook his head. "Borrmann did."

Allison swung around to Borrmann. The ex-town marshal was standing nervously between the table and the door. "Where?"

"Beside the trail, just inside the canyon, Clay."

Allison nodded, satisfied, then looked inquiringly at Borrmann. "Where the hell's my saddlebags — and my bedroll?" he demanded.

"In the barn, Clay."

"Don't 'Clay' me. Get them!"

"Sure thing."

Borrmann turned and disappeared out the door.

Allison went over to the bedroom door and opened it and went into the room. A single kerosene lamp sitting on the chest of drawers beside the bed was lit, casting a pale, flickering light on the figure huddled on the bed. He could see the ends of the bandanna protruding from her mouth. Her eyes were wide, staring, as he approached — and for just a moment he thought she was dead. Then she began struggling.

He relaxed and bent to examine her. Rick had trussed her well. The rope around her wrists was biting pretty deeply, but she'd live. Rick had tied her ankles as securely as her wrists and then tied them together, drawing her legs up sharply behind her. He looked into her wide, furious eyes. She should have been terrified. Instead, she was ready to spit in his eye. And she probably would have if Rick hadn't stuck the bandanna in her mouth.

"Would you like some water?" he asked her.

She nodded, her anger fading somewhat.

He returned to the kitchen and went over to the sink. A tin cup was sitting on the sideboard. He threw out the coffee grounds, then held the cup under the pump spout, filled it to overflowing with icy-cold water and returned to the bedroom. Joanne did not struggle against the rope as he approached her this time.

He stopped beside the bed and looked down at her, the cup of cold spring water in his hand. He saw her large dark eyes focus gratefully on the cup. Earlier that day those same eyes had snapped at him coldly, while her tongue had whipsawed him in front of Cody's townspeople like he was just some cur dog not fit to lick her boots.

He tipped the cup and let the water pour down onto her face and shoulders, then turned and left the room, closing the door firmly behind him.

The two punchers were standing just inside the doorway as Borrmann hurried into the kitchen with Clay's gear. Clay took his war bag from the man, fished out the stub of a pencil and an old envelope.

"Put that gear down," Clay told Borrmann. "I got a letter for you to write."

"Me?"

"You heard me. Beecher knows my handwriting."

Clay looked at the two cowpokes. "Can

either one of you read?"

Smoke looked quickly down at the tip of his boots, then up at Clay, shaking his head. Toby shook his head also.

"Good. You're going to deliver this here note to Beecher for me. But you better go about it real careful-like. Beecher ain't going to like what this note says."

The two men shifted unhappily but said nothing. Clay turned his attention to Borrmann then and indicated a chair at the table with a thrust of his hand.

As the man sat down, Clay slapped the pencil down on the table in front of Borrmann, ripped the back off the envelope, then spread the blank piece of paper flat on the table so Borrmann could use it.

"Now, just write what I tell you," Clay told the man.

Borrmann glanced uneasily at the grinning Rick Warner, then took up the pencil.

\* \* \*

Haggard from anxiety and lack of sleep,

183

Carl Beecher stirred suddenly in the big leather chair behind his desk. He had heard something from the direction of the barn, the creak of a hinge perhaps. He shook his head and blinked the sleep out of his eyes and was surprised to see the first light of dawn filtering through his window.

He must have been asleep, then.

He got up quickly and strode through the empty house to the door and flung it open. In the cold light he saw Smoke and Toby leading their horses toward him, the cantles of their saddles heavy with bedrolls and other gear.

When they saw him, they stopped, looked quickly at each other, then mounted and rode toward him.

"Where the hell you two been?" Beecher demanded.

Smoke pulled up in front of the porch and cleared his throat nervously. Toby, Beecher noted, was not able to look him in the face. He kept patting his mount's neck, his eyes downcast. Their behavior sent a warning shudder through him.

*They know something about Joanne!*

"Mr. Beecher," Smoke said, "we come to give our notice."

"Your *what?*"

"You don't have to give us what's owed for this month," said Toby, in a forlorn effort to placate Beecher.

"Why are you two running?" Beecher demanded.

"Anyway," said Smoke unhappily, "we got all our gear, so we'll be on our way, Mr. Beecher."

"Joanne's missing," Beecher told them bluntly. "She's been gone all yesterday afternoon and last night. She may be hurt somewhere. I'll need you and the other hands to search for her. You can't leave now."

"Yes, we can," Smoke said miserably, wheeling his horse about. "We just gave out notice."

If Beecher had had a gun on his thigh, he would have pulled it out then and fired a warning shot over their heads to make them pull up. "Come back here, you two!" he called.

Smoke looked back and pulled up. He moistened dry lips. "We met Kyle

Robinson on the way here. He gave us a note for you. I left it on the desk in the ranch office. You can't miss it."

He turned back around then in his saddle and urged his horse to a canter. When he overtook Toby at the gate, both men raised their horses to a gallop.

Furious, Beecher darted back inside, emerged a moment later levering a Winchester, and raced across the yard to the gate. Resting the barrel on the top rail, he sighted on the two riders. It was Smoke's back he caught in his sights first. Cold sweat broke out on his forehead. Then, with violent oath, he lowered the rifle.

He couldn't shoot Smoke or Toby. There was no way he could cut them down as they fled his wrath. He had known them, cursed them, and liked them too long for that.

Still carrying the rifle, he moved swiftly across the yard past the blacksmith shop to the north end of the bunkhouse and pushed into the ranch office. At once he recognized the sound of the squeaking hinge on the door as the same one that had awakened him not long before.

The desktop was rolled down and a wrinkled scrap of paper was sitting in the center of the writing surface. It seemed to have enormous, frightening significance as he crossed the small room toward it. Snatching up the piece of paper, he hurried over to the mud-smeared window and began to read:

*You burnt me out. Now I got yore dauter, if you want to see her alive agen, bring me $50,000 to the J Bar. Come alone. If I see any one else you wont see me and you wont see her agen. I am a desprate man.*

*K. Robinson*

Beecher's hand shook as he folded the note up carefully and placed it in his vest pocket beside the pouch of Bull Durham. *She's alive!* he told himself, clinging to that one fact in an effort to blot out all the other awful and soul-chilling possibilities that still crowded in upon him.

The doorway went dark abruptly and Beecher looked up to see Callahan. The big, swarthy blacksmith was leaning into the office with one hand resting on the doorsill above his head.

"Anything wrong, Mr. Beecher?"

"Why do you ask?"

"I saw you with your rifle a minute ago. Seems to me you weren't very happy with Smoke and Toby."

"You were awake?"

"They tried to get their stuff without making any noise, but the bunkhouse is wide-awake now. When two guys try to move around that quiet, they attract a lot of attention."

Beecher saw Andy crowding behind Callahan and heard the low voices of at least four of his cowhands as they spilled out into the gray morning.

"Never mind what you saw, Callahan," Beecher told the giant. "It's a personal matter — between me and them."

"Sure, Mr. Beecher." He pulled back out of the doorway.

At once Andy took his place.

"Miss Joanne still ain't back, Mr.

Beecher," he said nervously. "Leastways, her blue ain't in its stall."

Beecher nodded. "That's right. She's visiting with friends in town. Carol Bushnell."

"Oh." The horse wrangler didn't move.

"She sent back word with Smoke just now." Beecher walked toward the little old man. The fellow stepped out of the doorway. As Beecher closed the door behind him, he said, "I'll be riding into town myself before breakfast. Saddle the big dun for me."

"Sure, Mr. Beecher."

As Andy hastened back to the horse barn, Beecher — his face set grimly — strode across the yard to his big empty ranchhouse.

A little more than an hour later, Beecher guided his powerful horse across the creek where it coiled around a thick stand of willows. The horse found itself struggling for a moment in the deep mud, then it pulled itself up onto the bank and Beecher put the horse into the willows and dismounted. The willow grove was well in under the juniper-clad bluff that marked the western boundary of his land. In the center of the grove, a long, half-rotted log sat like a bench in the midst of a park.

It was a place Beecher had come to often after the death of his wife. Here, in complete and blessed privacy, he could bellow out his fury at the gods that tormented him — or sit with the music of the wind in his ears, healing the loneliness that left him raw at times.

He did not sit upon the log this time, however. Instead, he nudged it back with his powerful hands until he had exposed the dark, open soil of the ground beneath it. Taking out his huge Bowie, he dug a hole with swift, slashing strokes and with his bare hands pulled back out of the hole the dirt he had loosened. At last, satisfied that it was large enough to contain what he planned to deposit within it, he lifted the saddlebags off his horse and lugged them over to the hole and dropped them in.

Then he clawed the dirt back over the spot and rolled the log on top of the hole.

He had tried to keep the loose dirt over the long dark wound made by the rotting log and had succeeded for the most part. With the toes of his boots, he managed to scatter what fresh soil was visible. At last, satisfied that a casual traveler through this grove — and that in itself was pretty unlikely — would notice nothing unusual about the way the log sat, he mounted up and rode out of the willows, heading north.

He put his big horse at a full gallop as soon as he was clear of the creek.

## 9

Kyle was deep in troubled thought as he rode toward Carl Beecher's hacienda.

Finding Brad Borrmann, he now realized, was not going to be an easy task. Allison had disappeared, leaving Kyle with no leads at all as to Borrmann's possible whereabouts. The ex-town marshal had few if any friends left in town, since the power his post as marshal had given him seemed to have completely overwhelmed the man's meager wit. The result was that he had soon become a more frightening bully than those he had ostensibly been hired to curb.

Now, with the news of Tim Landon's death spreading throughout the territory, there was every likelihood that Borrmann had already fled south. If that were true, Kyle figured the one man left in the territory who might know where Borrmann could have gone was Carl Beecher — Borrmann's original sponsor and the man who had buffaloed the Cody town council into hiring Borrmann in the first place.

That was one good reason for Kyle to ride out and meet Beecher. But Kyle had others as well. He was curious to know the man who could breed so honest and fiery a daughter, while at the same time he was contriving to destroy or drive from the region every small rancher and homesteader that attempted to settle on his borders. And finally, Kyle had a grim personal desire to hold for a while the eyes of this man so that he might look deep into the soul of one who so willingly had been the principal moving force in the death of Jose and Mary Ramirez.

What Kyle would do after such a scrutiny, he had as yet no clear idea. But his promise to Jose was still a galvanizing urgency within him. It was a promise he meant to keep.

Cresting a small rise, still some distance from Beecher's ranch, Kyle caught sight of a lone horseman galloping across the grasslands in front of him. The rider was at least four furlongs in the distance and was heading almost due north. Kyle pulled up quickly and squinted at the rider. As the man rode, small hillocks occasionally came between them, so that Kyle found he had to stand in his stirrups in order to get a clearer view of the man.

The rider was wearing a dark suit, a clean white Stetson and was built powerfully about the chest and shoulders. He rode with a casual ease — the horse and man a single entity moving smoothly across Kyle's line of vision. Though from this distance Kyle could not tell the rider's age or pick out any of his features, something cold and certain within him told him that this was Carl Beecher — the man he sought.

Clapping spurs to his black, Kyle pulled swiftly around and took after the rider. It was a long, hard ride before he overtook the man; and when he finally managed to pull abreast of him, it was only then that the man became aware of Kyle's pursuit, so intent had he been on his forward momentum — so anxious was he to get where he was going.

But the moment he swung his head around and saw Kyle and the marshal's badge pinned to his vest, his face went dark with fury and he swung his horse toward Kyle. The two riders came together with violent suddenness, each one pulling back brutally on his mount's reins. The rancher's horse shook his head angrily and reared high on its haunches. Kyle patted his horse's neck as he circled the other horseman.

He was still not sure this was Beecher.

"You Beecher?" he called, still busy gentling his horse.

"You're Kyle Robinson," the man said, his voice hoarse with anger. But he too was having difficulty settling his big animal down.

"That's right, Beecher. And I'd like to ask you a few questions."

"You'd like to ask *me* a few questions?"

"That's right."

Beecher's powerful, craggy face darkened still further, in contrast to the unruly white locks poking out from under his Stetson.

Abruptly the man reached back and tugged at his gun. Kyle drew his own weapon with a swift, fluid motion, clearing leather before the rancher could get his draw well started.

"Hold it, Beecher," Kyle said softly.

Beecher held his hand on the butt of his revolver for a long moment. Then, slowly, he pulled his hand away and let it rest on the black wool of his trousers.

"Your note said *your* place, Robinson. And that it was money you wanted — not satisfaction."

The man's words made little sense to Kyle. "Speak plain, Beecher."

"Where's my daughter?" the man demanded. "What have you done with her?"

At once Kyle realized that Beecher's daughter had disappeared, with the result that the rancher was a deeply anxious man. Obviously Kyle had intercepted him in the midst of an attempt to locate his daughter; but why he should feel so strongly that Kyle had anything to do with her disappearance was a mystery to him.

"I don't know anything about your

daughter, Beecher. I'm after Brad Borrmann for the killing of Tim Landon. And I figured you'd be the man to tell me where I might find him."

The color in Beecher's face drained slowly. The man appeared to age before Kyle's eyes. "I knew it didn't figure. You just being made U.S. Marshal and all." The older man shook his head, then looked bleakly at Kyle. "How do you spell 'desperate,' Robinson?"

Surprised at the question, Kyle nevertheless realized that the man had a good reason for asking it. Without a pause he spelled the word for Beecher.

With no further comment, Beecher pulled a small, folded piece of paper from his vest pocket and handed it across to Kyle. Kyle took it, opened it and read what it said. Then he handed it back to Beecher.

"Glad I know how to spell 'desperate,' " Kyle said laconically. "I can also spell 'daughter.' You're right, Beecher. I sure as hell didn't write that note. And I had nothing to do with the kidnaping of your daughter."

"It's Clay Allison and his people," the man said. "I know that now. And Borrmann is probably tied in with them."

"You're riding now to give them the money?"

Beecher looked carefully at Robinson. "What I'm doing is my own business, Robinson. You got no love for me and I know why you're still in this territory, why that badge is pinned to your vest. Joanne repeated your threats to me. What I'm asking now is for you to back off and let me play this hand my way. Later, you can finish your business with Double B any way you see fit. I won't roll over for you, and I'll do what I can to give as good as I take. But there won't be anything crooked about it. All the cards will be on the table. Is it a deal?"

Kyle met the rancher's eyes and held them. He saw no treachery in them, no cold-blooded cynicism. All he found reflected in Beecher's steady gaze was wariness and fear — together with a soul-wrenching concern. That and a certain gallant defiance.

"You don't want me to tag along?" Kyle

said, dropping his six-gun back into his holster.

"You read the note. I'm to go alone."

Kyle nodded. "All right, Beecher."

Beecher almost thanked Kyle before he clapped spurs to his dun. The big horse was at full gallop almost at once. Kyle watched Beecher ride north, his coattails flying out straight behind him. Abruptly, Kyle urged his horse forward, cutting across Beecher's trail and quartering to the northwest, heading toward the mountains.

\*     \*     \*

The sight of J Bar's burnt-out cabin and outbuildings caused Beecher to appreciate Kyle Robinson's anger with a depth he hadn't felt before. This realization was promptly shut away, however, at sight of Brad Borrmann riding toward him from behind the blackened wreckage of the barn.

Guiding his dun through the creek, Beecher put his horse up the bank on the other side, then reined in on the flat to await Borrmann. He had been correct, he realized grimly, in figuring Borrmann to be in this with the others. And of course it was Borrmann's barely literate hand that had written that note — at Clay Allison's direction, Beecher no longer had any doubt.

Capping his indignation at having to treat with this contemptible underling, Beecher sat his horse and watched Borrmann pull up beside him. The man was unsure of himself, full of uneasy bluster as he hailed the rancher:

"Howdy, Mr. Beecher. See you got Robinson's note, all right."

"You mean Clay Allison's note," Beecher said coldly. "Now, where's my daughter?" He looked quickly around, settling at last on the cottonwoods north of where the J Bar barn had stood. She could be in there now, he realized, astride her horse with Allison beside her.

"She's safe, Mr. Beecher. But she ain't here. You just hand over the money and we'll send your daughter on her way."

"Swine," Beecher said softly, "what makes you think I would hand over fifty thousand dollars on the strength of your word alone? I want to see Joanne."

Sweat broke out on Borrmann's forehead. It was plain he had not been prepared for this eventuality. Seeing his distress and uncertainty, Beecher reached back swiftly and drew his big Colt. As Borrmann looked down the long barrel, he involuntarily reined his horse back a few steps.

"Unbuckle your gunbelt, Borrmann, and let it drop."

Borrmann hesitated only for a second, then began to tug on the buckle. As soon as the gunbelt and holster struck the ground, Beecher indicated with a quick movement of his gun that Borrmann should lead the way to wherever Joanne was being held.

Borrmann pulled his horse around and started to ride along the creek past the cottonwoods, following a well-worn trail, one that had been beaten into the ground by not one or two, but by countless herds of cattle. This then was the route his rustled cattle had taken as they were driven off his land by that Mex. No wonder the man had clung to this valley with such tenacity.

And yet, where could the greaser have taken the cattle by going in this direction? Years before, while searching out the boundaries of his land, Beecher had scouted this trail and others like it that led into the mountains. Each time he had returned satisfied there was no way to get his beef through these towering ramparts to the mining towns on the other side, since all the trails he had found petered out into blind canyons, most of which were locked in almost year round by ice and snow . . .

They were still moving along the creek, passing a heavy stand of cottonwoods, when Beecher heard the snort of a horse behind him. He turned in his saddle and started to bring around his Colt.

"Don't try it," said Clay Allison.

Clay's six-gun was aimed at Beecher's head, and the sheriff was less than ten feet from Beecher, his horse steady under him. Beecher paused. What he wanted more than anything else was to insure Joanne's safety, and he couldn't do that if he was dead.

"Drop the gun, Beecher," Clay

said. "Now."

Beecher let his hand open. The Colt struck the ground and skittered under his animal's feet. Beecher heard Borrmann riding back toward them.

"Thought you'd never make your move," Borrmann said testily to Allison. "What the hell kept you?"

"You," said Allison, his voice mean. "Wanted to see you squirm." Clay looked back at Beecher. "What you trying to prove, Beecher? Where's the money?"

"I don't have it with me."

"Now, just what the hell is that supposed to mean?"

"Exactly what I said. You won't see any of it until I see Joanne safe."

"You think we're going to let her go free before you come up with the cash?"

"The money's hidden where you won't find it. But I'll draw you a map as soon as I know that Joanne is all right."

Allison regarded Beecher suspiciously. Then he holstered his weapon. "How do I know you won't have me digging up half the Double B spread looking for that cache, map or no map?"

"Leave someone to guard Joanne and me. When you return with the money, you can release us."

Allison nodded, a shrewdness lighting his cold eyes. He looked over at Borrmann, who had dismounted and retrieved Beecher's six-gun and stuck it into his belt. "You go first, Brad. Mr. Beecher here will follow you. I'll just hang back to keep an eye on the old fox."

Borrmann swung into his saddle, urged his horse around and started up the trail ahead of them, a look of undiluted pleasure on his beefy face at this change in Beecher's fortunes.

As the rancher followed Borrmann, he felt a little better. He had not expected to be able to ride into Allison's camp without trouble. This way, Allison was escorting him safely to Joanne, and the deal — apparently — had been made with Allison, one he would have had to make in any case.

*　　*　　*

Kyle sat his horse quietly. He was in the same clearing from which, not long before, he had witnessed Allison's men besieging Jose. As he watched Beecher and Borrmann in the valley below him, he noted with a barely audible grunt the swift movement that brought Beecher's six-gun from its holster. Then, moments later, he watched Allison approach the unsuspecting rancher through the cottonwoods. Kyle considered firing a warning shot. But the impulse was only a fleeting one, to be discounted the moment it occurred to him.

He watched as Allison covered Beecher while the two men palavered. It was plain by this time that Beecher was not going to fork over any ransom until he knew Joanne was safe. When the three continued on up the trail, Kyle took a deep breath. As he had hoped, he was going to be given an opportunity to beard all the lions in their den.

He pulled his horse back from the lip of the clearing and started down the trail to the valley floor.

## 10

Smoke said, "Sonofabitch," softly, almost reverently, and threw his cigarette to the ground. He and Toby were standing in the cottonwoods below the burnt-out cabin, their mounts out of sight in the timber behind them.

With some pleasure they had seen Beecher draw on Borrmann and were watching as Beecher forced Borrmann to ride ahead of him up the trail that followed the creek. They were almost out of sight when Smoke saw another rider — Clay Allison — above the timber line, screened from the trail below by the juniper and scrub pine. From his vantage point Smoke could see Allison riding carefully toward Beecher and Borrmann as he kept the timber between himself and the men on the trail below him.

"That Allison's about to take Beecher

from his blind side," Smoke said unhappily.

"They ain't nothin' we can do about it," said Toby.

"I know it, damn it! That's just the problem."

"Let's ride out, Smoke. You know what Allison told us. He was right. We've run out our string here."

Smoke knew his partner was right. They sure as hell *had* run out their string in this country.

"You shouldn't a read that note, Smoke," Toby went on, shaking his thin head sadly. "We'd be long gone now if you hadn't."

Smoke glanced at his partner. Smoke had lied when he told Allison he couldn't read, so naturally he had read the note the first chance he got. The result was he had muddied up his resolve something fierce.

"I know that, Toby. But it ain't doing you no good to keep on reminding me of that. I read it and that's that. Thing is, I never figured Allison and Warner would treat Joanne like that. And I sure as hell never counted on them asking for ransom before they'd let her go."

"So Beecher'll fuss some, but he'll pay. Hell, Smoke. He's got the money — and then some. He'll get her loose."

"I hope so," Smoke said, turning back into the cottonwoods.

"We going to ride out now?" Toby asked anxiously as he followed after his partner.

Smoke untied the reins that tethered his horse to a sapling and swung into his saddle. Looking down at Toby, he nodded. "Guess so, Toby. But I'd sure as hell rest a lot easier if I knew for sure that little girl used to ride on my saddle horn was going to be all right."

"She ain't been a little girl for a long time, Smoke."

"She growed up tough as old leather, and that's a fact," agreed Smoke. "But I still keep thinking of her as that same little girl with the big eyes. Guess that's my problem."

Toby swung aboard his own horse. "Hell, Smoke. I feel like you do. But they just ain't nothin' we can do now but ride.

And that's a fact."

Smoke took a deep breath and peered out through the trees at the trail Beecher and Borrmann had taken earlier as they moved north past the burnt-out buildings. What he felt was shame, he realized. Shame for allowing those men to treat Joanne the way they had. And shame at the way Allison had spoken to them and then sent them on their way. And the way they had packed their gear, like two thieves in the night, then galloped out through the gate of the Double B, leaving Beecher alone to find that note on the desk.

Smoke glanced over at Toby. It was Toby Smoke was thinking of. Toby was ten years older than Smoke and no longer the man he once was. They had their nest egg now and could ride north to that little horse ranch they'd been talking up now for the last five years. It was sitting up there just waiting for them. And for Toby it was coming just about in the nick of time. Yessir. Toby was a stove-up cowboy ready now for a rocking chair on a porch — his own porch, at last. Toby needed it and he deserved it.

And pretty soon, Smoke realized, he would need that rocker himself. So maybe he wasn't only thinking of Toby, at that.

He felt a little better coming to that conclusion and was about to pull his horse around and lead the way out of this valley when he heard the sound of a horseman descending the steep trail that led from the bluff overhead. Holding his hand up as a warning for Toby to be quiet, he spoke soothingly to his horse to keep it from whinnying to the stranger's horse as it passed close by the cottonwoods.

Looking out through the trees, he caught a fleeting glimpse of a lean rider with a badge on his vest, riding a big, powerful-looking black. As the rider gained the far side of the stream, it was obvious to Smoke that he was following Beecher's sign.

"That's Robinson," Smoke told Toby. "He's after Beecher — and the others too, I'll bet."

"How do you know?"

"From the descriptions I been getting from the other hands. And from that badge on his vest. Remember what Allison said about Robinson being made a deputy U.S. marshal?"

"I forgot," said Toby. He looked back out at the rider. "Now what?"

"I don't know. I just don't know. Mebbe this gent will pull our chestnuts out of the fire."

"Why, sure," said Toby, brightening considerably as he watched the solitary rider move past the charred and blackened wreckage of what had been the Mex's ranch. "So we don't need to worry no more. Right, Smoke?"

But Smoke did not reply. He sat his horse quietly and reached for his sack of Bull Durham. He needed a smoke to sort things out in his mind. It had just occurred to him that even though this feller was now the deputy U.S. marshal, he sure as hell didn't have no love for Carl Beecher — or for anyone connected with the Double B. And that included Joanne Beecher.

Smoke built his cigarette slowly, thoughtfully.

They were past the tree line, a chill wind in their faces, when Clay Allison pulled up.

"Hold it, you two," he called to Borrmann and Beecher.

Borrmann swung around in his saddle and looked past Beecher at Clay. "What is it, Clay?"

"I heard something."

Quickly dismounting, Allison pulled his Winchester out of its sleeve and hurried back down the narrow trail until he got a clear view of the mountainside. The trail seemed empty enough, at least that portion of it visible through the scrub pine. Not satisfied, however, he crouched down on one knee, leaned over the edge of the trail, and listened.

A tanager darted suddenly from a twisted limb below him, uttering a sharp *prit-ik!* Its cry echoed and re-echoed above the cool sound of the creek rushing just below him on its way to the valley floor. Then the bird fluttered out of sight, leaving only its sharp cries echoing in the narrow gorge. As the last of the bird's notes faded, Allison heard once again that sound he had caught earlier: the steady click of iron shoes on stone.

As he had thought — a lone horseman was tracking them.

Not long before, Borrmann had insisted on pulling up. His mount was favoring its right-front hoof. It had turned out to be a small pebble wedged between the horse's hoof and the shoe. The animal had been skittish, however, and it had taken a little while for Borrmann to pry the pebble loose. As a result, whoever was moving up that trail behind them had no notion just how close to them he now was.

Clay smiled, then got to his feet and hurried back up the trail to the others. The best part of this was he had a pretty damn good idea just who this tracker might be.

"What is it?" Borrmann asked, as Clay reached for his horse's reins.

"We got company," Clay answered shortly, stepping into his saddle.

"Company? Who the hell is it?"

Borrmann was obviously alarmed.

"How should I know? For sure, that is." He smiled wolfishly at Borrmann. "But maybe I got a pretty good hunch who it is. And if I'm right, he's in for a real surprise."

Borrmann swung into his saddle and both men waited for Beecher to mount up as well. As the rancher settled into his saddle, Allison said to him, "Keep your mouth shut now, Beecher. If this is who I think it is, you'll have no good reason to stop me."

Then, with Allison following, Borrmann and the rancher rode on up the trail. Clay was looking for an impregnable, well-hidden position that would command a clear view of the trail for at least twenty yards. And when at last he found the spot he was looking for, it did not matter to him at all that almost each move he now made was a duplicate of similar moves he had made a month earlier. Nor that this time Beecher himself was a witness.

Clay pulled up.

Borrmann and Beecher did the same. Borrmann looked back at him. Allison pointed to a pile of boulders heaped before a large wash to their right. "Get in behind there, Borrmann, and keep the horses out of sight. There's grass back in there. That should keep them quiet. And be damn sure you keep Beecher quiet."

Borrmann and Beecher dismounted. Borrmann unlimbered his six-gun and prodded the rancher ahead of him between the boulders, both men pulling their horses in behind them. Clay waited until they were out of sight, then moved in after them. He slapped his mount on the rump. When his horse caught sight of the other mounts cropping the grass further in, she trotted happily toward them.

Borrmann, his revolver trained loosely on the rancher, was a few yards back, watching Allison closely. When he caught Allison's eye, he grinned suddenly. He and Clay knew something old Beecher didn't.

Allison levered a fresh cartridge into the firing chamber of his Winchester, turned around and rested the barrel of his rifle on the rocky shelf before him. There was complete silence for a while, except for the ghostly roar of the rushing creek just below the trail.

At last, above the sound of the water, Allison heard the steady clop of a horse. A moment later the rider he had expected emerged from behind a leaning shelf of white rock. Robinson's impassive face was soberly intent as he focused his eyes on the trail before him. He carried himself slack in the saddle, leaning slightly foward to save the big, handsome black. And so far he suspected nothing.

Allison snugged the rifle's stock into his shoulder, leaned and sighted along the barrel. The sheriff was aiming for Robinson's chest, the center of it. As Robinson rode closer, Allison's sight caught the man and he began to track him. Abruptly Allison heard the dim sound of a scuffle behind him, followed by the crack of bone on flesh. Something hard and metallic clipped to the rocky ground.

Turning his head swiftly, Allison saw Beecher rushing across the few yards that separated them, both hands reaching out to grab Allison. Swinging himself around completely, Allison crouched to receive the rancher's charge. As soon as Beecher was close enough, Clay brought his rifle stock up and around in a swift arc that caught Beecher flush on the side of his head with such force that the man's head flipped over and both his legs flew out from under him. He struck the ground just in front of Allison, his body out flat, both arms flung loosely like rag doll's, his head crunching down upon the hard ground. He lay where he had fallen without moving a finger, as still as a dead limb.

Furious at this complication, Allison looked back and saw that Robinson had pulled up sharply and was looking in his direction. Flinging the rifle up to his shoulder, Allison sighted quickly and fired. He saw Robinson's head tug back and his hat fly off. The man clutched convulsively at his reins. His black reared high and Robinson tumbled back off his horse, disappearing over the trail's rim. The horse almost went over with him, but managed to scramble back onto the trail. Then — riderless — it bolted back down the trail.

Allison ran out from the rocks and across the trail. Leaning out over the edge, he looked down at the creek and saw Robinson being swept along in the fast water. Only his head and shoulders were visible, and as Allison watched, Robinson's body folded limply about a huge boulder and then was swept headlong through a narrow channel.

Getting swiftly to his feet, Allison levered another cartridge into the firing chamber and squeezed off a shot at the twisting body. He did not see the small geyser of water that would have indicated a miss and concluded hopefully that he had sent still another slug into the body of the new U.S. Deputy Marshal.

Borrmann, rubbing his chin ruefully where Beecher had struck him, was beside Allison by this time. He had seen the shot and his eyes were gleaming with appreciation of it.

He handed Allison Robinson's hat. "Look inside."

Allison took the hat and turned it over. A dark-crimson stain covered the sweatband and a good portion of the crown.

"You really got him good," Borrmann said. "That second shot wasn't even necessary."

Allison flung the hat out over the creek and watched it for a moment as it spun down toward the water. Then he turned and hurried back to where they had left the rancher.

Beecher was still sprawled where Allison had knocked him.

"Too bad the sonofabitch didn't see that first shot of yours, Clay," Borrmann said. "It was as sweet a shot as the one that caught Jed."

"Shut up, damn you!" snarled Allison.

Allison had seen the rancher stir the moment Borrmann started speaking. Now, in dismay, he saw the man shake his head like an old bull and look up in fury at Allison.

"You . . .!" he muttered thickly. "It was *you* killed my son!"

The rancher started to scramble to his feet. He was still groggy from the blow to his head and stumbled twice before finally making it to his feet.

Allison had been waiting calmly. The moment Beecher started for him, Allison moved in swiftly and struck him unconscious with a single vicious swipe of his six-gun.

As the rancher dropped, Allison turned on Borrmann.

"Goddamn you, Brad! That mouth of yours is going to cost you! There ain't no chance in the world we can let Beecher go now. Not after he knows I'm the one killed his boy." Allison looked back down at the fallen rancher. He shook his head. "He's a dead man."

"Hell, Clay! I thought he was still out."

"Don't make no difference now," Clay said, shrugging. "Tie him onto his horse. He's still got to draw us that map, don't forget."

Borrmann swallowed unhappily as Clay left him to get his horse. He guessed Allison was right. Beecher would follow them both to hell — and further — no matter how much money or time it took. So — like Allison said — that meant they would have to . . .

Borrmann blinked away the unpleasant thought and bent down for Beecher's limp body.

# 11

Kyle had caught the glint of sunlight along the barrel of Allison's Winchester a split second before the rifle's crack. The bullet struck him above his left eye just as he started to dismount. The slight movement of his head at this moment was undoubtedly what saved his life, since the slug — instead of crashing into his skull frontally — sliced a furrow along his forehead and glanced off.

Nevertheless, the impact had the force of a crowbar as it smashed his head around and flung him back. He remembered his hat flying off, the chin strap ripping brutally past his nose and over his head. He tried to hang on to the reins but only succeeded in pulling the horse back. It reared and he felt himself falling.

He came down on the back of his shoulders with numbing force. He clutched dimly at the outcroppings of rock and the roots of the scrub pine that poked out from the mountainside. But his punishing, tumbling fall was only slightly broken as he plunged finally into the icy waters of the creek. The shuddering cold of the water shocked him to wakefulness and as he was swept along he looked up at the trail far overhead and found himself wondering how he had managed to get so far from it in such a short time.

And then he was under the water, being pulled rapidly along. Gasping for air, he found himself plastered against a huge boulder that blocked his progress a moment before the rapid current plucked him off the rock and sent him past it through a narrow channel. A faint shot from far overhead sounded and he saw a portion of the rock splinter and disappear and heard the sharp whine of the bullet as it ricocheted away. At once he ducked under the water and let it carry him past the rock.

But once through the channel, his progress became somewhat swifter and not at all gentle. He was dropping along

223

with the water, skimming over rocks, occasionally slamming into them with numbing force. When he tried to regain some control, he found himself unable to muster the strength — and then he was plunging down almost vertically.

He started to tumble, but before he could make a complete turn he knifed into a deep pool. The cold this time was paralyzing. A swift undertow caught him and dragged him still deeper into the icy waters. Abruptly, the buffeting ceased. But the cold seemed to have sapped him of all volition and he made no effort to help himself as he began drifting down, away from the light, turning lazily — like something spent. Or something dead.

The thought startled him. He began to pull toward the light. The pain in his oxygen-starved lungs was excruciating, yet no matter how hard he struggled to reach the surface, he seemed as far from it as before. Then, dimly, he felt hands grabbing at the collar of his shirt. Another pair of hands caught his vest. He broke through the water and opened his mouth blindly, gulping air hungrily, and felt himself being dragged onto land like some enormous fish. The lids of his eyes were ponderously heavy. He had no strength left to open them and seemed to want only to escape the awesome cold by burrowing still deeper into his body.

Rough, powerful hands began to slap him in the face. At first he resisted the anger this treatment aroused. But the insistent blows continued without letup until he suddenly found himself reaching up to ward them off. His eyes flew open and he twisted his face away.

At once the punishing hands ceased their pummeling. Like someone becoming reacquainted with a body he had recently abandoned, Kyle blinked the water out of his eyes and peered up at the two men looking down at him. His head was throbbing violently and a dark-red tear was creeping down over his left eye. He shook his head to clear it away, but he had little success.

"You look like hell, mister," said one of the men. "How do you feel?"

Kyle felt his mouth twist into a faint smile. "Like hell, of course.

And damn cold."

The fellow turned to his partner. "Get that fire going, Toby."

"Sure, Smoke," Toby replied as he turned and hurried from the shore and began snatching up firewood.

Toby was obviously older than his partner and seemed almost as insubstantial as the dried-out twigs and branches he began dumping to the ground beside them.

Smoke looked back down at Kyle. "Cold, you say?"

Shivering, Kyle nodded.

Smoke took off his wool-lined jacket and dropped it over Kyle's shoulders.

"Thanks," Kyle managed through chattering teeth. Again he tried to brush away the growing patch of blood that hung down from his left eyebrow.

Smoke unfastened Kyle's bandanna, dipped it into the stream, and wiped Kyle's forehead clean. He rinsed the bandanna and then held it against Kyle's wound.

"Here," he said. "Hold it there. You got a nasty crease, but seems like you'll live. How's it feel?"

"Like a mule's kick."

Smoke nodded. "We'll have you warm in a minute." He glanced at Toby, who was bent prayerfully over the pile of brush, willing the fire into life as he held a flickering sulphur match in under the pile. A puff of blue smoke was followed by a tiny *whoof* and flame poked hungrily up through the wood. The sound of it snapping at the dry wood was a fabulous music to Kyle. Still holding the wet bandanna to his forehead, he pulled himself closer to the fire and let its warmth seep into his bones . . .

*      *      *

Joanne had heard the horses approaching the ranchhouse and then the sound of Allison's voice in the next room as he entered. She turned her head with some difficulty and faced the door. With Allison back she could breathe a little easier. Rick Warner had been coming in more often and staying longer each time, and the hunger in his eyes had grown more fierce with each visit. Only her implacable hatred had kept him from handling her.

They had taken the bandanna out of her mouth, but they had not untied her and by this time she had lost most of the feeling in her hands, and her back — constantly arched as it was — ached terribly.

But now Allison was back with the money and she would be freed.

Clay Allison's heavy footsteps approached the bedroom door. The door swung open. Clay's heavy figure filled it for a moment and then he stepped back and out of the way. A second figure entered the bedroom — Brad Borrmann — and he was carrying someone over his shoulder.

*Her father!*

"What have you done?" she gasped.

"It ain't us," said Allison, approaching the bed. "It was him. He got fancy. Wanted to see you before he told us where his money was hid."

Borrmann pulled up beside Allison, breathing heavily.

"Put him down beside her," Allison told the man. "Then untie her."

Allison looked at her. "He's all right. He'll have a real mean headache for a while, I suppose. But he ain't dead, if that's what's worrying you."

Borrmann ducked forward, dumping her father's limp body onto the bed. It jounced under the rancher's six-foot frame, causing the rope to bite still further into her wrists. But she didn't care about that. All she could think of was how still her father looked as he lay face down on the bed beside her.

As Borrmann took out a knife and moved around the bed to get behind her, she looked at Allison. "He was your friend. Haven't you done enough to him? Did you have to treat him like this as well?"

"None of this would have happened if he'd just brought the money like the note said."

Borrmann's knife sliced through the rope that had drawn her legs up behind her. At once she straightened and felt a sudden, excruciating cramp in her left side from the sudden exertion. She gasped. Borrmann pulled her wrists toward him. She felt the cold steel of his blade as he fitted it in under the rope. And then he slashed up through the ropes. She pulled her hands around and began to rub them frantically as Borrmann cut loose her ankles. Sharp pins and needles swept into her hands and into her feet, down even to her very toes. Never before had she felt them this severe.

But she ignored her discomfort as she turned her father over onto his back. At once she saw the cruel welt on the side of his head. When she bent to examine it, her left hand inadvertently traced still another head laceration, this time on the top of her father's skull. A ridge at least half an inch high had been raised.

"You butcher!" she spat with barely suppressed fury as she flung a look back up at Allison.

Allison shrugged and backed away from the bed. "I'll leave it to you to bring your father around. He promised us a map to where he hid that money. So let me know when he's ready to draw it. Just sing out."

He paused to watch her bend anxiously back over her father. She did not appear to be listening to him as closely as she should.

"Just remember," he finished harshly, "the sooner we get that money, the sooner you and him can go back to the Double B."

He waited for her response, but she was too intent on examining the scalp laceration she had just discovered. Allison turned and walked from the room, Borrmann leaving with him. As soon as the door was pulled shut behind them, Joanne turned up the lamp on the battered chest of drawers alongside the bed. Her hands still tingled angrily and she did not dare attempt to support herself on her feet, but her concern now was focused entirely on the condition of her father.

She bent close to him. "Father! Can you hear me?"

Joanne saw a muscle on the man's face twitch, and then — slowly — he turned, opening his eyes.

"Don't tell them," he whispered hoarsely. "If they know I'm all right, they'll want the map."

"Shh!" she told him. "Lie still."

Carefully, surprised by the pain it

caused, she pushed herself off the bed and stood upright. For a moment she thought she would pitch forward, but she forced herself to take a step. The pain lessened somewhat and she was pleased to see that she was walking.

In a moment she had reached the door. She pulled it open and looked into the kitchen. Allison, Rick Warner, and Borrmann were sitting at the table, nursing a jug and playing cards with a worn, greasy deck. At the sound of the door being pulled open, Allison glanced up and the others swung around.

"I need towels and cold water," she told them, "to wash off his face, to clean away the dried blood." She spoke these words bitterly, accusingly.

"We ain't got a towel," said Rick Warner, smiling at her wolfishly. He swiftly untied his bandanna and held it out to her. "Use this. There's water at the sink."

As she started toward him for the bandanna, Allison cocked an eyebrow.

"He's awake now, huh?"

"No," she said bitterly. "He's still

unconscious. How could you have beaten him so cruelly — a man his age?"

"Hell, he's got plenty of pepper for a man his age. He came at me, he did. I didn't have no choice. You say he's still out?"

"You heard me," she said, taking the bandanna from Rick and turning to the sink.

She found an earthenware bowl, dropped the bandanna into it and filled the bowl with water from the pump. As she started back to the bedroom, Allison got to his feet and blocked her passage. She stopped and looked up at him defiantly.

"You're in my way," she told him.

"Don't you let him play dead, Joanne. He's a tough old buffalo. If he don't come around pretty soon, I'll slap him awake. And that won't be so nice. You wash him off and soon as he opens up those eyes, you let us know. There ain't no sense in you two trying to make this any tougher then it has to be."

She moved firmly around him without comment. Once into the bedroom, she leaned back against the door as she closed it and took a deep breath. Then she hurried across the room to the bed. Her father stirred as she sat on it beside him.

"Shh!" she said softly. "Just stay quiet and let me clean off your wounds." She began to wipe away the dried blood and dust from the side of his head.

Without moving his lips, he whispered, "They killed Jed. I heard them talking. Clay Allison did it."

Joanne pulled her hand back as if her father had struck her. At once she found herself asking why she had not suspected Allison. Then she thought of the Mex — and Kyle Robinson. As she tried to collect her thoughts, she blurted, "But why?"

"Don't know," her father whispered. "Don't know. They killed Robinson too. I tried to stop them."

Blindly, her mind in a turmoil, she leaned forward again and began dabbing at her father's face. She felt as if she were in the midst of an incredible nightmare, into which she kept falling deeper and deeper with each passing moment.

She heard the door open. Without

turning, she kept dabbing at her father's discolored cheek until the heavy footsteps paused behind her.

"He still out?" It was Allison.

She did not dare trust herself to speak to the man. She wanted to fly at him, to rake his face with her fingers. Instead, she kept dipping the bandanna into the cold water and wiping at her father's face. Her control was not so great, however, that she was able to prevent her hand from trembling. "See for yourself," she managed tightly.

He moved around her and bent close to her father. "Hell, I didn't think I'd hit him that hard."

"You hit him more than once. He's got a terrible welt on the top of his head."

"Yeah. So I did. Damn." Allison straightened and looked down at the still form on the bed. He was obviously worried for the first time that he might have caused a serious injury when he struck her father.

He turned to her abruptly. "You two stay in here for the night. Rick'll bring in some beans. Let me know when he comes around."

She nodded.

He looked at her closely, as if he were trying to find any trace of forgiveness in her eyes. She had been aware for months how he felt about her and had gloried in making sure he knew just how she felt about him in return. She had not been kind. Watching his eyes now as he studied her, she did not regret any of it. Indeed, it gave her great comfort. All she wanted now was to be able to punish him — to kill him, even — for the murder of her brother.

Afraid that her anger would surface and reveal too much, she looked away from Allison and back at her father.

"I'm sorry it had to be this way, Joanne," Allison said.

She did not reply.

"I mean, the two of us — we could've maybe — "

"Get out of here!" she hissed, turning on him, eyes blazing. "Just leave me with my father. I find you loathsome! Is that clear enough for you!"

He backed away from her quickly.

It was as if she had struck him. His face hardened and without a word he turned and strode swiftly from the room.

As soon as the door was pulled shut behind him, she dropped her face into her hands and began to sob silently.

*   *   *

It was dark now and the campfire blazing up sent a bright halo of light into the pines that crowded the shore and out onto the rushing stream beside them. Overhead the moon, as bright as a silver dollar, hung in a cold sky.

Kyle was almost completely dry now. His horse had been recovered by Toby, and Smoke had retrieved his hat when he had caught sight of it floating down the stream soon after they pulled him from the water. His wool-lined jacket had been taken from his bedroll and thrown over his shoulders. His bandanna had been wound tightly about his forehead, Indian fashion, to staunch the flow of blood from his scalp wound. Except for a slight discoloration where the makeshift bandage covered the wound, the bleeding appeared to have stopped and all Kyle felt now was a dull, throbbing headache.

At first the two men had been reluctant to discuss their presence on the trail behind Kyle. But that was no longer so, and Kyle had just asked them bluntly why they had taken Joanne to the canyon ranchhouse, instead of going back with her to the Double B and facing the music.

"It wasn't just the rustlin' of Double B's stock," Smoke explained unhappily. "It was more than that — a damn sight more. The man woulda killed us, sure as shootin'."

"What else was it?"

Smoke took a deep breath, then plunged on, seemingly anxious to unburden himself. "Jed — Beecher's son. Allison kiled him, not that Mex. 'Course, Allison and Borrmann let Beecher think it was the Mex. That's why they dumped Jed's body just below the Mex's cabin — "

"His name was Jose," Kyle said quietly. "Jose Ramirez. His wife's name was Mary."

"Sure, Kyle. Sure. Well, anyway, they

dumped Jed's body on Jose's land so they could blame him.''

"Why did Allison kill Jed?''

"Because Allison and his boys were the ones who was rustlin' Double B stock — along with the stock of all the other ranchers nearby. Oh, sometimes they'd leave Double B cattle on a small rancher's spread where they could find it. See? But most of the time they was the ones doing all the rustling. We caught them and made a deal. We'd keep our mouths shut and even help out as long as we could take our cut.''

"And Jed caught wise.''

"I guess so. The way Borrmann told it, they was hazin' some cattle up near the pass and found Jed on their trail. Allison bushwhacked him — just like he bushwhacked you. Only when they fished Jed out of the water, half his head was blown away.''

"I should consider myself real lucky, then.''

"You sure as hell should,'' broke in Toby. Then he leaned forward and dropped a new piece of wood on the fire.

"But Jose and his wife weren't so lucky, were they?"

Smoke had no comment on that. He just glanced nervously at his partner, then peered down into the fire. The tip of his cigarette pulsed as he pulled the smoke deep into his lungs. In the campfire's bright glow Kyle could see the lean, leathery planes of Smoke's face setting into a mournful cast. The man obviously regretted his hand in that ugly business.

Indeed, had he not felt this remorse, he would not have followed after Beecher and then, later, after Kyle himself. Kyle owed his life, then, not only to Smoke's concern for Joanne's safety but also to his uneasy awareness of what misery his and Toby's betrayal had helped bring about for Double B.

Strangely, Kyle could not bring himself to generate any real anger toward these two old cowpokes. They had seen a bleak future stretching before them. Too stove-up for regular work as ranchhands, the most they could look forward to was riding the chuck lines until they wore out their welcomes and then, if they were lucky, finding jobs as roustabouts or wrangling horses for other men to ride. In hopes of something better, they had thrown in with Allison.

"Did Jose know anything about this?" Kyle asked. "After all, this trail goes right through his spread."

"We was mighty careful," said Smoke, "but I got an idea it was Jose who put the bee in Jed's bonnet."

"That's right," said Toby. "I saw them two in town just before they found Jed. They was in a corner of the hotel bar, talking real quiet. Jed was sure as hell listening with all ears, he was."

"So Allison killed Jed, then had Borrmann dump his body on Jose's land and lead Joanne and the posse right to it."

"That's the way I figured it happened," admitted Smoke gloomily. "From what Borrmann let on yesterday at the canyon ranch."

"You hadn't figured it before this?"

Smoke looked nervously at Kyle. "I had a pretty good idea, I guess."

Again, Kyle found himself unable to generate any great anger. He felt only an overwhelming weariness with these good men before him.

"Where's that ranch?" Kyle asked.

"You won't find it tonight," Toby said.

"It's hid real good," said Smoke, "on the other side of the pass. It's a good long ride from there too."

"Tell me how to get there."

"You ain't gonna hurt Joanne, are you?" Toby wanted to know.

Kyle looked at them both coldly. "I thank you fellers for pulling me out of the drink. Now you just let me do what I have to do. What maybe both of you woulda done if you'd had the sand."

Toby glanced shrewdly at Smoke. "Or been a mite younger," he volunteered.

Smoke's shoulders slumped. "Tellin' where it is ain't so easy. And finding it still ain't goin' to be as easy as you figure. You better listen careful."

"I will."

Smoke took a stick from the pile alongside the fire and began to draw in the sand. Kyle paid close attention. Smoke was right, he realized. Finding this canyon wasn't going to be easy.

# 12

Joanne moved swiftly to the window and peered out through the dirt-encrusted panes.

For most of the morning, she and her father had been menaced periodically by first one, then another of their three captors. They were convinced that she and her father were deceiving them as to the seriousness of her father's head injury. Of the three, Rick Warner took the most delight in his crude efforts to poke and shake her father into consciousness. Twice Joanne had had to pull him away from her father. Now, thank heavens, with the arrival of four strange horsemen, the attention of Allison and his men had been diverted as they went outside to meet the newcomers.

Greeting Clay cheerfully, the four riders swung down out of their saddles and started toward the house with Allison and his men. Two of the newcomers were roughly dressed range riders Joanne had never seen before. The two others were cut from different cloth, however. They seemed a good deal more prosperous, judging not only from the quality of their mounts but from the clothes they wore. One of them, the smallest of the four, was wearing a bowler hat and was passing out cheroots as he walked toward the ranchhouse.

The men disappeared from Joanne's sight and a moment later she heard them tramping into the kitchen. The scraping of chairs followed as they settled themselves around the table. Moving to the door, she was able to hear snatches of their conversation.

At first she had hoped she might be able to attract the attention of these newcomers, who might be persuaded to turn on Allison and the others and release her and her father. But as she listened to the rough banter that passed between them, she realized how slight a chance there was of this.

They were cattle buyers, come to bargain for the cattle that has been rustled by Smoke and Toby. The haggling did not last long and it was obvious to Joanne that these men had done business before, regularly. The cattlemen knew what they were buying, and as a result their offering price was distressingly low. Only a token argument was raised by Allison, however, the price moderately adjusted and a bargain quickly struck.

The men went back outside to inspect the cattle, all but Rick Warner, she noticed. Borrmann was carrying a jug of moonshine and passing it among the buyers. They were making a party of it, she realized, and returned to the bed.

"You can sit up," she told her father. "They're too busy selling our cattle to bother us for a while."

Her father slowly sat up. "All of them?" he whispered.

"Rick Warner is still in the kitchen, I think."

He nodded grimly.

"Let me take a look," Joanne said. "They've all been drinking. Warner's awful quiet in there. Maybe he's passed out at the kitchen table.''

He looked at her with sudden hope in his eyes. "I'll go," he whispered.

"No," she insisted. "Let me. You're supposed to be unconscious still, don't forget. If Rick catches me, I'll just tell him I want some water."

Her father sighed and nodded. The bleakness in his eyes returned. "Just be careful. Of all Allison's men, I trust him the least."

Joanne nodded. She felt the same way about Warner. She left the bed and approached the door as softly as she could manage. Lifting the latch carefully, she pulled the door back slowly. When it creaked on its hinges, she froze and held her breath. But when there was no outcry — no sound of any kind — she pulled the door open far enough to enable her to peer into the kitchen.

Rick was sitting at the table with his back to Joanne. His head was resting forward on his arms and just beyond his head was a stoneware jug. Listening carefully, she was sure she could hear

Rick's heavy breathing.

He had passed out!

He was still wearing his hat but it was pushed well back on his head. His holster hung down over the seat of his chair, the butt of the six-gun to her. It was that weapon she wanted. Swiftly, she glided into the room and crossed to the table. Reaching down, she yanked the heavy weapon from Rick's flapless holster.

Immediately Rick sat up and turned around, a broad grin on his face. Joanne took a quick step back, brought up the weapon and with her left hand thumbed back the hammer. Pointing at Rick's grinning features, she took another step back.

Rick got up swiftly and started toward her, the careless grin on his face confusing Joanne.

Taking another step back, she said, "Stop right there, Rick Warner! I'll shoot! I'm warning you!"

"Go ahead," Warner said, pulling up. "Pull the trigger, Miss Joanne. Go on! Pull it!"

"You don't think I will?"

"Oh, sure. I think you will."

She studied his face. It dawned on her then that he had come awake rather swiftly. He had obviously been drinking, but his cold eyes experienced no difficulty in focusing and he was remarkably steady on his feet for a man who just a moment before had seemingly passed out. She caught the mockery in his face now, the pure insolence. He brushed back his long, greasy blond hair and smiled more broadly than before, revealing his imperfect, yellowing teeth. They struck her as being more fangs than teeth, and she took another step backward, the enormous revolver trembling in her grasp.

Rick took a quick step toward her and she knew he was about to wrest the gun from her. Closing her eyes, she tugged on the trigger. The hammer snapped forward onto an empty chamber. Before she could cock the gun a second time, Rick had snatched it away.

Furious that he had tricked her, she rushed at him, her hands like claws, intent on raking her fingernails down his face. But Rick ducked almost casually to one side and brought an open hand around swiftly, catching her flush on the right cheek. The harsh blow yanked her head around violently and Joanne felt herself slam back against the wall.

Before she could get her bearings, Warner moved closer and slapped her twice — snapping her head first in one direction, then backhanding her face around the other way. The kitchen reeled about her as she sagged to the floor. She became dimly aware of Warner standing over her, that frightening, evil grin on his face. Then he reached down, grabbed the front of her dress and hauled her roughly to her feet.

"I been lookin' forward to this, Missy," Warner spat, leaning his stubbled face close to hers. He smiled. "Yessir, takin' you down a peg is gonna be a real pleasure!"

Then he flung her brutally against the wall. The back of her head struck sharply and she felt a sob break out of her throat.

And then — with a cry like an enraged animal — her father flung himself out of the bedroom upon Warner, bearing down upon the man with such suddenness and fury that it caused Rick to stagger back. But only for a moment.

Twisting away, Rick flung her father from him. The man, obviously weakened considerably, staggered awkwardly against the table and almost slipped to the floor. As he grabbed the table for support, Rick brought up his six-gun, aimed coolly and squeezed the trigger. The sound deafened Joanne and she saw a chunk of the table close to her father's hand disintegrate as the slug tore into it.

Rick thumbed back the hammer and aimed a second time. "Next shot'll be some closer, Beecher," Rick said. "I won't kill you. I'll just wound you a little."

At that moment, from outside the ranchhouse came the explosion of many hoofs and the bleating of cattle. The rustled beef was being driven off by the cattle buyers. The sound of the bawling cattle filled the room, causing the building's foundation to tremble. Joanne looked across the room at her father. He met her gaze, and she saw in his eyes a sudden hopelessness. The sound of the moving cattle was like an ominous harbinger of what was to come. And more than that: a proof of their helplessness.

Rick saw the look on their faces and laughed. "Yep, there they go," he said. "The last of the J Bar cattle Smoke and Toby brought in, along with some of your stock, Beecher." He glanced out the window at the clouds of dust that now obscured the barn and the pens behind it. "It sure was nice of you to pay us for rustlin' your cattle."

Joanne saw her father's shoulders slump. She looked at Rick Warner. "You won't get away with this!"

"Why not? Who's going to stop us?"

She thought then of Kyle Robinson's death and realized that Rick was correct. There was no one left to stop them. It was strange, she realized — and not a little ironic — that she should feel this pang once again at the reminder of Kyle Robinson's death . . .

The door opened and Allison strode in, Borrmann close on his heels. "Well, well," said Allison. "I see Beecher's up and about." He grinned at Rick. "It worked just like I said it would, huh?"

Rick nodded, dropping his six-gun back into his holster. "Soon's I let on I passed out, she left the bedroom and came after me. When I caught her, Beecher came awake real fast."

"We heard a shot."

"Just a warning to Beecher here." Warner glanced at Joanne and grinned. "Bet you're wonderin' why my gun wouldn't go off for you. Hell, Miss Joanne, it just ain't good sense to carry a gun inside with the next firing chamber loaded — case you have an accident, see?"

Joanne felt suddenly drained. They had all been so far ahead of her. She watched her father, glaring defiantly at Allison, slump into a chair at the table.

"You can kill me, Allison," her father said. "But I'm not drawing you a map. Not until I see Joanne ride out of here."

Allison walked over to the table and looked down at his former partner. "Hell, Carl, you ain't got no choice in the matter." He glanced quickly at Joanne, then back at her father. "We figure you could take any punishment we could dish out — and then some. But what about your daughter, Carl? And then again, we just might be nice to her. Know what I mean? She may be a mean, spiteful bitch and all that — but she's a nice lookin' filly, I'll have to admit. And Rick here's taken quite a shine to her. Not to mention Borrmann. You want me to draw you a picture, Beecher?"

"You . . . animal!" Joanne cried.

Allison spun about and walked heavily across the floor toward her. He stopped just in front of her, reached around with one hand and grabbed a fistful of her hair and wrenched her head back violently. The pain was sudden and intense and she found herself staring helplessly up at the ceiling. She heard her father's cry and the sound of his chair scraping as he lurched to his feet to go to her aid. There was a short scuffle, followed by the sound of her father's deep, painful grunt. Then she heard him being flung back down into his seat.

"Now you listen to me," said Allison,

his voice hoarse with a sudden, seething rage. "You've treated me — all of us — like we was dirt under your feet! You were too good for us! We were just hired scum your father brought up here to do his dirty work! You treated us like we didn't have no feelings!" He flung her violently back against the wall. She struck it smartly and found herself staring back at him with stinging, tear-filled eyes. "Sure! Maybe we're animals!" he snarled, breathing heavily, his voice thick with emotion. "But even animals have feelings! And before we're through with you, that's what we're gonna turn you into. We're gonna make you just like us! *An animal!*"

"Allison!" her father cried, struggling to his feet despite the efforts of Borrmann to keep him down. "Enough of that. Leave her alone, I say. I'll tell you where the money is. You don't even need a map."

Allison spun about and hurried back to the table, eyes gleaming.

"You know that willow grove near the creek," her father told him, "the one in under the bluff. You've met me there once or twice."

Eyes narrowing in sudden comprehension, Allison glanced around at Warner and Borrmann. "Sure," he told her father. "I know the place."

"The cash is in saddlebags, buried under the log in the clearing."

Allison looked at her father for a long moment, obviously trying to figure if he was lying or not.

"I'm telling you the truth, Clay," her father said. To her astonishment, she saw tears gleaming in the man's eyes. "For God's sake," he pleaded, "take the saddlebags and ride out of this country. You've taken my son from me — shamed my daughter, beaten me. What more do you want? Take the money and get out."

The old and beaten man's plea seemed suddenly to shame Clay Allison. He turned and, avoiding Joanne's eyes, spoke sharply to Borrmann. "Get them back into that room. See they stay there."

Joanne hurried to her father's side and helped him move back across the kitchen to the bedroom. She paid no attention to Borrmann's clumsy hands on her back as he pushed her into the room. As soon as the door was pulled shut behind them, she breathed a deep sigh of relief and led her father to the bed.

\* \* \*

Clay Allison sat down at the table and reached for the jug. As soon as the door closed behind Joanne and her father, he unstoppered the jug and took a long swig. Rick sat down across from him and reached for the jug himself.

"What are we going to do with them, Clay?"

"We can't let them go. They'll have half this territory on our heels. Beecher's still a big man in these parts."

"He don't look so big now," said Borrmann, joining them at the table and reaching for the jug.

"That don't make no difference. We maybe took him down a peg, at that. But once he's outa here, he'll get on his high horse pretty damn fast. You can count on it."

Warner nodded agreement. "You're

right, Clay. If we let him go, we'll have to hightail it all the way to Mexico. And even that won't be far enough, I'm thinkin'."

Borrmann shrugged and wiped his mouth with the back of his hand. "So what do we do?"

"You," said Clay, "will go out tonight and start digging a hole. A big one. Big enough for the both of them."

"Me? Where?"

"Find a spot, damn it."

"I'd rather not, Clay."

"I see. You'd rather pull the trigger on them, is that it?"

"I didn't say that."

"Well, damn it, that's all the choice you got."

"I'll dig the grave. I know a good spot just off the trail. Alongside Frenchie."

"That'll be fine," said Clay, reaching for the jug. "Rick and I will see to them — and afterward we'll see to this place."

"What do you mean?"

"We're going to burn all this down. The barns, this house, the pens. Before noon tomorrow we'll have that money and be on our way south — with no one the wiser."

"A lot of people are going to wonder what happened to Beecher and his daughter."

"Let them wonder. There ain't no law against that. They'll never find this canyon — not from the other side of the range, they won't. And there won't be nothing left standing here to connect us with their disappearance."

"What I don't like is having to kill them both," said Borrmann. "I mean I hate thinking about it. Know what I mean?"

"Shut up," said Allison, taking another swig from the jug. "Just shut up and stop thinking about it. All you got to do is dig a hole."

"Yeah," said Rick, grinning suddenly at Borrmann. "Just figure you're making as a new privy."

In spite of himself, Clay grinned at Rick. If you had to think about it at all, he supposed, that was maybe the best way to look at it. You had to keep a sense of humor at time like this.

# 13

Kyle was astonished. And maybe just a little upset as he found himself, astride his horse, staring up at a solid wall of rock, the stream he had followed this far trickling through a long narrow fissure in the canyon wall. There was no chance at all that the ranch Smoke had mentioned was on the other side.

All that morning Kyle had followed the trail that led over the pass. Early that afternoon, as Smoke had said he would, he had come to another stream and followed it, on the lookout all the while for a ledge off to his right under which a fork of the stream had cut a second channel. Following this second channel was supposed to lead to the hidden canyon. But somewhere behind him, Kyle had missed the ledge.

Kyle pulled his black around and started

back up the stream.

It was almost two hours later when Kyle found once again the spot where the cattle had been driven off the trail and into the stream's rocky bed. The water was fast and crystal-clear at this point. With the pebbles and small stones that made up the stream bed leaving no obvious reminders of a small herd's passage, this trail had been a perfect one for rustlers. But they had used this stream recently and Kyle could not believe that the swift water had washed away all sign or that the gravel and sand had filled in every hoofprint. He got off his horse and, leading it, began to walk down the shallow stream, his eyes alert for any impression in the sand, any sign of crushed or striated rock.

Gradually his eyes became alert to every unusual mark and disturbance in the stream bed, signs he had overlooked when first he had ridden through. Striated rock, tiny crushed fragments, and occasional hollows where cattle had foundered began to leap to his attention. Soon he was following the trail J Bar's cattle had left as easily as if he were following their hoofprints on dry land. That he had not done this earlier — relying instead on Smoke's deceptively simple directions — pained him somewhat as he pressed on through the swift, icy water.

And then, abruptly, the signs of the herd's passage vanished. Kyle pulled up, turned and looked back upstream. He saw no ledge. The shoreline was crowded with stunted cedar bushes and a thick, high grass, dun-colored now and withered. Behind the cedars stood a thick stand of lodgepole pines completely shielding the white rock face of the canyon wall behind them. Along the shoreline two rotting pine trunks were resting in among the cedar.

But where was the ledge under which the water had cut a channel that led into the hidden canyon?

He pulled his horse around, slogged up onto the shore and was about to start back up the stream a second time when he caught the gleam of something metallic in among the pines. He pushed his way past the bordering brush, reached down and picked up a spur. The entire spur had been left behind: the heel band, spur strap, and rowel. The spur button had been torn off and the heel chain broken.

Dropping to one knee, Kyle examined the ground. The pine needles left little trace, but Kyle was sure he could make out two slight furrows in the ground, one of which ended in a small depression — at the point where he had found the spur. The owner of this spur had been dragged past this spot, losing his spur in the process. And that meant he must have been in pretty bad shape not to notice it or stop to retrieve it. A working cowboy was a near-useless being without his spurs.

Of course, a dying cowboy was no longer in any condition to worry about such matters. His working days were over. Kyle recalled Frenchie then, stood up, and looked ahead of him beyond the stand of pines. Still pulling his mount after him, he walked out of the pines and found himself suddenly aware of a trembling under his feet.

Dropping to one knee, he used the spur's rowel to dig through the carpet of pine needles. It did not take him long to reach the sandstone beneath it. Tipping his head just a little, he listened. The sound of swift running water just ahead of him was barely audible above the roar of the stream behind him.

He had found the ledge.

Pulling his horse quickly after him, he soon saw once again the muddy tracks of countless hoofs on the ground ahead of him. In a few more yards, the pine needles from the lodgepole stand behind him had petered out completely, revealing the beaten trail. And further ahead he could hear clearly the driving roar of another stream as it cut its way toward the canyon's rock face. And then the sandstone ledge appeared, raw and white, jutting out of the ground — and under it the swift stream of water emptying into a deep gully that cut sharply through the soft red earth.

Pausing beside the narrow stream, Kyle looked back along the shelf of rock and saw where it followed the shoreline behind the pines until it reached in under the bed of the stream, well above the pines. Overlaid with gravel and sand, he had missed it completely as he continued on down the stream past the pines. And he would have missed it going back.

Yet, once a rider knew where it was, it was almost impossible to miss. No wonder this canyon ranch of Clay Allison's had remained hidden for so long. The setup was damn near perfect.

He started down the stream and saw at last, not two hundred yards further down the slope, the fifteen-foot-high cavern that had been worn through the rock face by the stream. Beyond it, he knew, was a clear trail into the hidden canyon and the ranch.

Kyle pulled up and let his horse crop the grass beside the stream as he took out his sack of tobacco. He was tired. His shoulders ached almost constantly. That fall from the trail had not been the best medicine in the the world for a gunshot wound, and his head still throbbed like a dull toothache. His boots were sopping wet from walking so long in the stream, and his feet were like ice. Even so, things were likely to get one hell of a lot worse before they got much better, so Kyle took full advantage of what he knew would be his last chance to relax.

He was careful with the finely cut tobacco, anxious not to lose any of it as he sprinkled it along the rice straw paper. His tongue worked quickly, without disturbing any of the tobacco. He sealed it, lit the cigarette with a sulphur match and dragged the smoke gratefully into his lungs. Above him in the tops of the pines the wind sighed, and at his feet the stream ran. As the peace and wonder of the place seeped into his soul, it caused Kyle to contemplate the violence of these past weeks — and the violence that awaited inevitably beyond that cavern before him.

Turning back was unthinkable, but when he thought of Smoke and Toby waving goodbye to him as they rode back down the trail, he found himself envying them just a little bit. They were escaping with their ill-gotten gains, as the Sunday preacher would call it, but Kyle could no longer find it in him to blame them. Worn-out cowpokes didn't ordinarily have much to look forward to when they could no longer climb aboard a bronc without wincing. He was glad those two had that ranch. At least that was something.

The hard, chattering note of a mountain bluebird broke into his thoughts. Kyle glanced skyward and saw the turquoise bird bolt from the pines and veer up the face of the canyon wall. To Kyle it was a reminder that it was getting late.

He dropped what little remained of his smoke, ground it out and reached for his horse's reins. As he stepped into the saddle, he let fall the spur he had picked up in the pines. It had served its purpose. Kyle had no doubt now to whom it had belonged.

Frenchie Wells.

As Kyle knew from Smoke, Frenchie had died as a result of Kyle's shot. Kyle wished he was a just a little sorry. But he wasn't. For now that left one less gun between him and Clay Allison. And Beecher.

For, after all, a promise was a promise. And Kyle had promised Jose to get them. All of them.

Night was falling fast as Kyle tethered

his black well off the trail and kept going on foot down the slope to the floor of the canyon. The ranch buildings were huddled on the far side of the canyon, the faint yellow light of kerosene lamps filling the window squares and brightening the raw ground about the ranchhouse. The large cattle pens in back of the barns caught Kyle's attention at once.

It sure as hell had been a slick operation. And Beecher, it seemed, had paid for it. All the way.

Kyle paused. He heard the sound of a spade striking stone. Someone was digging in the ground off the trail. He drew his six-gun, crouched and tried to make out from which direction the sound was coming. The spade was working steadily. Kyle could hear it slicing cleanly into the soil, occasionally striking rock as it did so.

Peering into the gathering darkness off to his left, Kyle caught a steady, regular movement just behind a clump of juniper. Still keeping low, he cut through the brush toward the working figure. The sound of digging grew louder with each step he took. And whoever was digging was so intent on his job that Kyle found himself able to move close in behind him, duck behind a tree, and then peer around it at the man and at the considerable hole he was opening in the ground in front of him.

Abruptly the fellow stopped, pulled a bandanna from his hip pocket and mopped his face with it. It was Brad Borrmann, Kyle realized. And it was not a hole he was digging.

It was a grave — a pretty damn big one.

"Just hold it right there, Borrmann," said Kyle softly, stepping out from behind the tree, his six-gun trained on the man's ample gut.

The man's face went white with shock. He had been in the act of grabbing up the spade by its handle. Now he clung to it for support.

"That's right. I'm not dead," Kyle told him quietly, stepping closer. "Who's this grave for? It sure as hell is big enough."

Borrmann seemed to shake off his surprise and his face hardened into resolve. Kyle saw the man's knuckles tighten on the handle a second before he brought the spade up and around in a sweeping arc aimed at Kyle's head. Unwilling to alert the ranchhouse with a shot, Kyle ducked under the spade. The blade knocked his hat off, but Kyle stayed down and hurled himself at Borrmann, hitting him in the chest with his left shoulder and driving the man relentlessly back.

With a frightened gasp Borrmann toppled backward into the hole he had been digging, Kyle right on top of him. The fellow struck hard and was momentarily stunned. Kyle sat up and brought his six-gun around smartly, clipping Borrmann on the side of the forehead. Borrmann's head snapped around, then lay still.

Climbing out of the grave, Kyle retrieved his hat and looked down at the unconscious man. Kyle had nothing with which to bind and gag the man, and he wanted to keep the ex-marshal out of any further action for a while. Tugging his hat down firmly, Kyle reached for the spade and began shoveling the loose dirt piled beside the open grave back in on top of

Borrmann. Kyle had no love for the man — especially when he thought of what Borrmann had done to Tim Landon — and it would not have been a difficult thing for him to cover the man completely. If any of this gang deserved to be buried alive, Borrmann did. Nevertheless, Kyle was careful to leave the man's head uncovered.

In a moment most of Brad Borrmann's bulk was out of sight underground, a mound of fresh earth marking the site of his burial. With a grim smile, Kyle tossed the spade aside and started again for the ranchhouse.

It was almost completely dark now.

\* \* \*

Allison and Rick were sitting at the table, a blackened kerosene lamp shedding a fitful light, an earthenware jug in the center of the table. Night had come swiftly and with it a chill typical of this high country.

Clay reckoned it was about time. If they was ever to get out of this cold country, they'd better start moving now. He reached back and pulled the cards out of his hip pocket.

"We gonna use your cards?" Rick asked, his eyes narrowing.

"That's right. You got any objections?"

"Hell, no. Why should I have any objections to you using your own cards, Clay?" Rick reached for the jug and hooked it expertly over his shoulder. He took a couple of hefty swallows and slammed the jug back down on the table. Grinning, he wiped his mouth with the back of his hand. "So what the hell difference does it make anyway? You've already got me figured for the job."

"I told you. We'll draw for it."

"Sure."

"I mean it, damn it!"

Clay slammed the deck of cards down on the table between them.

"High card rings the bell," said Rick.

"Low card."

Rick leaned back and looked at Clay closely. "I said high card, Clay. And I called it first."

"Cut, damn it."

"What is it? High card or low?"

"Have it your way. High card and you get the brass ring."

"I'll cut, then."

Rick cut the cards. Clay put the deck together and shuffled. The sound of the cards snapping seemed to fill the room like thunder. Beecher and his girl were in the other room on the bed, trussed like Christmas turkeys, waiting with their heads down on the bed. Rick had seen to that. This way, as Rick had explained with a grin, they'd hear whoever it was enter the room, hear the footsteps getting closer . . . and closer . . .

"You gonna shuffle them cards forever?" Rick wanted to know. "You'll wear 'em out."

"You're pretty damn anxious."

"Ain't you?"

Clay shrugged and slapped the cards down on the table between them. "Go ahead."

Rick cut the deck and held up his card. It was the ace of spades.

"No need for me to cut," said Clay, feeling as if someone had taken all the air out of him. He was relieved — and that was a fact. Then, looking across the table at Rick, it occurred to him that Rick was not a bit unhappy. Hell, he was elated!

Smiling broadly, Rick reached for the jug and took another belt. "I get the brass ring," he said, wiping his mouth.

Astonished, Clay said, "You were anxious, all right. You were afraid I was going to get the high card."

"That's right. I sure have come to hate that girl and her old man. We was just dirt under their feet. This will be a pleasure. But I can't figure you, Clay. You shoulda been as anxious to get the call as I was."

"That's all right," Clay said, shuddering involuntarily. "You won it fair and square. Some guys just have all the luck. You going to use your hands — or your six-gun?"

Clay's sarcasm was lost completely on Rick as he considered seriously Clay's question. "A six-gun. Saw a guy get strangled once. It takes forever. Surprisin' how much strength a feller can muster when he feels fingers tighten on his throat."

Clay reached for the jug. "Yeah, sure. Well, get to it, then. Brad should be back any minute, and we got the barn and this place to fire yet."

Rick pushed his chair back and got to his feet. Lifting his six-gun from its holster, he spun the cylinder to check its load, then moved toward the bedroom door, a gleam in his eyes and a smile on his face that convinced Clay he was right in going through with what he had planned.

They had already poured considerable kerosene over the floors and walls of the barn, and a wagonload of hay saturated with kerosene and coal oil was waiting to be rolled against the ranchhouse. Clay's intent was to catch both Borrmann and Rick inside the ranchhouse and fire it.

He didn't see any sense in sharing all that money with a fool and a nut.

# 14

Kyle had just finished easing himself over the windowsill and lowering the sash when he heard heavy footsteps approaching the bedroom door. The trussed figures of Beecher and Joanne were outlined dimly on the bed, and his intention had been to free them first and enlist their aid in capturing Clay Allison and Rick Warner.

But there was no time for that now. Kyle darted across the room and flattened himself against the wall behind the door. Just as he felt the wall against his back, the door swung open and someone strode in. Whoever it was did not close the door behind him as he started across the room toward the bed.

Kyle stepped out from behind the door and saw Rick Warner approaching the bed with a six-gun glinting dully in his right hand. Warner's intention was obvious.

And even as Kyle started across the floor to overtake Warner, the man's arm leveled as he took aim at the back of Beecher's head.

A board creaked under Kyle's foot. The sound of it gave Warner pause. His gun hand wavered. By that time Kyle was within arm's reach. He brought the barrel of his Colt down on Warner's head. But the man had started to turn. Instead of coming down squarely, the barrel glanced off the side of Warner's head, ripping away a piece of his left ear and crunching brutally down upon his shoulder.

With a barely audible groan, Warner collapsed at Kyle's feet. But the man was not unconscious. His right arm and hand were still healthy and he retained control of his gun. Rolling over on the wooden floor with desperate fury, he brought up his gun and fired at Kyle. The gunflash illuminated the dark room with stark, livid light, and the reverberation from the shot caused the floor to dance under Kyle's feet. Kyle felt the hot slug whisper past his ear and thunk into the ceiling over his head.

He strode swiftly forward and kicked the Colt out of Warner's hand. It slammed against the wall behind Warner. The acrid smell of gunpowder caused Kyle's nose to twitch and his eyes to smart. He reached down through the white smoke and hauled Warner to his feet. The man tried to pull away. Kyle brought the barrel of his gun around. This time he caught Warner on the side of the face, the force of the blow causing Warner to go flying headfirst into the wall beside the bed.

Unconscious, he crumpled to the floor.

"What the hell?"

Kyle spun. Clay Allison was standing in the doorway.

"Who the hell's in there? That you, Brad?" Clay demanded.

Allison took a step into the room, drawing his six-gun as he came. Kyle dropped to one knee and brought his Colt around.

"Drop it, Allison," Kyle told him.

The man froze.

"I said drop it."

With a convulsive movement Allison shoved his gun hand forward and squeezed off a shot. Kyle felt the crown of his hat lift. He rolled swiftly to one side, getting off a quick shot. The gunflash blinded him momentarily in the darkened room, and when he blinked and looked again the doorway leading to the kitchen was empty. A second later, Kyle heard the outer door open and slam shut.

Kyle scrambled to his feet and raced out into the kitchen. Pushing open the outside door, he was greeted with fusillade that splintered the door and ripped out portions of the doorjamb. He pulled the door shut and ducked to one side. Slugs started spraying through the shattering windows. Keeping low, Kyle ducked back into the bedroom.

The two bound figures on the bed were struggling convulsively. Kyle could imagine their terror. The thunderclap of six-guns firing in such close confines, amplified to a shuddering intensity by the walls and the bare floor, must have turned their souls to jelly. Swiftly, he untied first Joanne's bonds, then her father's.

"It's all right," Kyle told them.

He helped Joanne to sit up. She looked

at him with wide, staring eyes as she rubbed her hands together in an effort to restore circulation.

Beecher stared with haunted eyes at Kyle. He too rubbed his hands together, but slowly. He seemed unable to comprehend Kyle's presence. "I thought you were dead," he said in a hoarse whisper. "They . . . talked about it . . . how they shot you . . ."

"That's what happened, all right. But Smoke and Toby fished me out."

"Smoke? Toby?"

"I'll explain later. Right now, Allison's got us pinned down in here." He glanced over at Warner's six-gun lying against the wall. "Can you use a gun?" he asked Beecher.

The man nodded.

"Take Warner's. Maybe you can cover me while I try to break out of here."

The man nodded and got up slowly. Stepping over Warner's crumpled body, he picked up the six-gun and looked at Kyle. It was as if he wondered for the first time at Kyle's motive — especially considering what Kyle's mission in this country had become. He swallowed. "You're throwing in with us, Robinson?"

"For now, I guess," Kyle admitted.

Beecher nodded, as if that made complete sense to him. Then he stepped back over Warner's body and, crouching, approached the bedroom window.

"I see gunflashes from the barn doorway," Beecher said.

"Stay there and keep him busy. I'll try to sneak out through the kitchen door while he's answering your fire."

Beecher nodded and poked out the windowpanes with the barrel of his weapon. Kyle took Joanne by the arm and pulled her toward the room's inner corner, the spot least likely to catch stray bullets. She was surprisingly meek and pliant to his touch, her eyes still wide with terror.

Abruptly, Beecher started firing out the window at Allison. Kyle crouched and ducked into the kitchen. Keeping low, he opened the door a crack and peered out. Beecher's firing had driven Allison away from the front of the barn, it appeared.

The diversion had worked. Kyle began to push the kitchen door open wider when he heard Joanne's shrill, horrified scream from the bedroom. Kyle turned to see a wild-eyed Rick Warner plunging through the bedroom doorway toward him, the left side of his face and most of his long, stringy blond hair livid with blood. There seemed to be something wrong with his neck and his left arm hung loosely by his side. But he came at Kyle with a brutal impetus born of desperation, bowled Kyle over, flung him out of the way and rushed out the door.

Lying flat on the floor, Kyle saw Warner lope crookedly across the yard toward the barn. Abruptly a fusillade coming from one of the barn windows cut Warner down. The man dropped to his knees, tried to get up, and then received a second withering outpouring of lead from the same opening. Kyle aimed carefully at the flashes and squeezed off two quick shots.

The firing from the barn ceased and, to Kyle's surprise, a puff of flame appeared to envelop the window — almost as if his bullets had set the barn afire. He paused, waiting for more shots to come from the barn. Then, instead of gunfire, he saw a blazing wagon piled with hay erupt from the mouth of the barn. The barn was slightly above the ranchhouse and the slope imparted to the flaming wagon an increased momentum as it plunged toward the kitchen side of the ranchhouse. Kyle saw it cut down the still twisting Warner, dropping its blanket of flaming hay over him as it bore down relentlessly on the ranchhouse.

He slammed the door shut and hurried into the bedroom. Snatching Joanne by the arm, he turned to Beecher who was still crouched by the window, as if mesmerized by the onrushing wagon of fire.

"Back! Get back from that side of the house!" Kyle called to him, pulling Joanne out of the corner and against the far wall.

Beecher appeared to rouse himself. He got to his feet and started toward the wall where Kyle was crouching with Joanne. But he got no more than halfway across the room when the wagon struck. The entire house shook with the force of the collision. A portion of the wall closest to the kitchen collapsed inward and a sudden blast of heat rolled across the floor toward them. A glance through the bedroom doorway showed Kyle a brilliantly lit room with roiling tongues of fire sweeping across the floor.

The table and the windows behind it vanished in an instant. Black, dense smoke rolled in through the doorway, momentarily blocking out the leaping flames. The whole ranchhouse shuddered in the grip of the devouring fire.

"The window," Kyle gasped. "Out the window. The flames should shield us from Allison's sight."

Beecher looked at Kyle. Kyle found he had to prod the man. Dully, he nodded and led the way back to the window and lifted the shattered sash. Kyle took off his jacket and placed it down over the sill to protect Joanne as she clambered out through the window. Beecher was next. Joanne, holding one hand over her head to protect her hair from the searing heat, turned and helped her father pull his long frame out through the narrow window.

As the wall between the kitchen and the bedroom vanished in a ball of fire, Kyle climbed out after Beecher.

The two were huddled like terrified children on the ground before the window. Kyle snatched his jacket off the windowsill.

"Get around behind the house!" he told them. "The trees over there! Hurry up! You're not safe here!"

Beecher nodded with sudden understanding, took Joanne by the arm and pulled her along with him. Kyle saw them running at full tilt toward the pines behind the house. In a moment they disappeared into the stand. Kyle shrugged into his jacket, checked his six-gun and headed toward the barn. The heavy jacket shielded him from the fierce heat, but all he could hope to protect him from Allison's bullets was surprise.

Smoke was pouring out of the windows and lofts of the barn and flame was licking through its sides as Kyle approached. He was less than five yards from the main door when four horses bolted out of the barn. They were too wild with fear to see him. Kyle dodged the first two, but the third caught him a glancing blow, hurtling him to the ground. The fourth horse galloped straight over him, his hoofs missing Kyle's head by inches. As the storm of horses passed beyond him, Kyle started to get to his feet, and was just in time to see Allison, aboard a powerful dun, charge out of the barn, heading right for him.

Kyle crouched, waited until Allison was almost on him, then dodged to one side and leaped upward, catching Allison's right arm and hooking his own about the man's elbow. As the horse galloped past, Allison was lifted from the saddle. He tried to beat off Kyle's grip, but as he leaned over to do so, he was yanked from the horse and tumbled down upon Kyle.

Both men hit with numbing force, Kyle landing on his wounded shoulder. The spasm of pain that swarmed out from it temporarily immobilized him as Allison rolled away from him and staggered to his feet. But the thought of Allison getting away from him now aroused Kyle as nothing else could have. He had dropped his gun in the effort to pull Allison off his horse. There was no time now to retrieve it.

Scrabbling toward Allison on all fours, he managed to lift himself just enough to get both feet driving under him. He hit Allison headfirst in the midsection. The man did not go down, however. He kept his feet and staggered back, beating down upon Kyle's head and shoulders with both fists. But Kyle kept driving and in a moment he realized that both of them were enclosed in a scorching frame of fire. Kyle had driven Allison back into the barn.

With a cry of terror, Allison tried to break free of Kyle's encircling arms. Reaching upward, Kyle caught the man's neck, wrapped one arm around his head and pulled Allison to the floor of the barn. His right arm was almost numb by this time, and all he could think of to do was keep Allison with him in this inferno until both of them fried.

But Allison was too terrified to be held. He twisted free in a wild, convulsive movement, then slipped on a patch of smoking hay and went tumbling backward into a stall. Kyle regained his feet and was about to start into the stall after Allison when the man emerged with a pitchfork in his hands. His face contorted with fury and terror, he drove at Kyle with the pitchfork.

Kyle was just able to fling up one arm to ward off the tines. A beam wrapped in flames plunged down out of the loft and crashed to the floor behind Kyle. Ignoring it, Kyle tackled Allison, knocking the pitchfork out of his hands and pulling him to the floor.

Shouting, Allison started beating at Kyle. Kyle pulled him closer and tried to bring his left arm around to encircle Allison's neck, but his wounded shoulder sent him rigid with pain. His head began to spin sickeningly . . .

Allison broke loose, scrambled to his feet and began to run. He took no more than three steps to the barn entrance before a second huge beam crashed through the loft. It struck Allison a glancing blow and knocked him sideways into another horse stall. As if it were a signal, the wall of hay piled behind the stall exploded into flame and instantly Allison and the stall ignited with a dull *whoomp!*

Allison's screams aroused Kyle. He staggered to his feet and started toward the blazing stall. But before he could reach it, Allison bolted from it — a plunging, animated torch — and raced blindly past Kyle out into the night.

Beating at the flames that licked at his boots and portions of his clothing with one hand, Kyle shielded his eyes with his other arm and raced out of the barn after Allison. He caught up to him, tackled him, and began rolling him over on the ground, unmindful of his own blistering hands as he did so — and without questioning his frantic effort to save a man who but a few moments before he had wanted only to kill.

As Kyle struggled with Allison, he heard running footsteps behind him and a moment later felt the shuddering impact of first one, then another bucketful of water. Most of the water drenched Allison, turning the man into a sodden, smoking ruin. Kyle looked up and saw Beecher and his daughter, two empty buckets in their hands. Behind them the barn was a crackling inferno. Kyle realized they must have gotten the water from the horse trough in front of it.

Slowly Kyle got to his feet and looked down at the whimpering, blackened figure sprawled face up on the ground. Allison's face was raw, his eyebrows gone, his eyes staring sightlessly up at them as his blistered lips worked feebly.

Kyle looked at Beecher. "He's burnt bad, but he'll live, looks like."

Beecher looked down at the smoking, still twisting form of the man who had murdered his son and shook his head. "No," he said bitterly, "he doesn't deserve to live! He . . . " Then his voice broke and he turned to Joanne, who reached out to comfort him.

As she did so, she glanced over at him and frowned with sudden concern. "Your eyebrows are gone," she said. "You've been burned too."

Abruptly, a cry — or rather a drawn-out, terrified wail — erupted from the pines on the other side of the canyon. It was an unearthly cry, wrung from a soul catching its first glimpse of hell.

It was Brad Borrmann.

"That's Borrmann," Kyle remarked, smiling thinly at Joanne. "I left him in the grave he was digging for you two."

Joanne recoiled at his words. Kyle looked at Beecher. "I'll be bringing Borrmann in for the killing of Tim Landon. Right now I suggest you two check what's left of the barn and ranchhouse for blankets and sheets. If Warner's dead, we'll need something to bury him in. And we'll need something to wrap around Allison when we take him in to Doc Fletcher."

Beecher nodded wearily; then he and Joanne started toward the still burning barn. It had collapsed in on itself by this time and was burning with much less intensity. Kyle glanced down at Allison. The man would not be going anywhere, Kyle realized. Kyle turned and started across the canyon toward the still wailing Borrmann.

As he walked, his spirits lifted somewhat. He was sore all over, his hands were blistered, and he wasn't sure if his eyebrows would ever grow back. But it was over. He had kept his promise to Jose — at least as much of it as Jose would have wanted him to keep.

# 15

Fresh mountain flowers were propped in front of each cross, Kyle noted, as he rode up onto the flat and approached the twin graves. He dismounted, left his horse and walked closer to the graves and took off his hat. As was his practice, he chose a spot just between the foot of both graves and bowed his head.

Kyle spoke then to the spirit of his friend: "I'm leaving this here high country now, Jose. There ain't no welcome left in it for a man who remembers as close as I do. Besides, it's all over now. I did what I promised you, *Amigo*. Still, I'd a damn sight rather have you back in that cabin working over your tally sheets. And Mary working up one of those extra fat tortillas she used to make. Hell, I can still taste them sometimes — when I'm riding along and see a cabin ahead of me with a light in the window . . . Well, then. This is goodbye. *Adios, Amigo*. You too, Mary."

Kyle took a step back, slapped his hat back on, then turned and walked to his horse. He swung into the saddle, took one last look at the two graves, then pulled his horse around and put it on the trail leading back down the mountain.

He was out of sight of the flat when he heard a horse overtaking him from above. He pulled up. In a moment Joanne Beecher rode down through the pines and gained the trail just behind him. He turned in his saddle and touched the brim of his hat as she rode alongside.

"I figured it was you put those flowers there," he told her.

"When I saw you coming, I knew you'd appreciate a little privacy."

"That was thoughtful of you. As a matter of fact, I had come to say goodbye."

"You're leaving?"

"Yes, I am."

They started up together and rode a ways in silence. Then she looked across at him. "Why? That J Bar land is yours now.

That's a fine spread and you have my word that the Double B will leave you in peace."

"That ain't it, Miss Beecher. I don't have the money to rebuild the place and restock it even if I wanted to, which I don't. This here country has grim memories, if you know what I mean."

Joanne nodded, and he could tell she understood perfectly. "I plan on hanging on to the Double B," she said. "I don't see why I can't run it myself."

"Don't see why not either. How's your father?"

She shook her head. "The same. It just . . . took too much out of him, I guess. He tries to take an interest in things. But . . . there's just nothing he seems to want. Except Jed back, I suppose. He'll never get over the fact that he imported and paid the killers who murdered Jed. He told me once he felt like it was his own gun that shot Jed." She shook her head.

"Reckon a man punishes himself a whole lot more efficient than the law can. Sometimes, that is."

She looked at him grimly. "Yes, I

suppose that's true." She frowned. "Then, you won't be staying for the hangings?"

He shook his head. "I reckon Judge Prescott can handle that end of it without my help. I just kept that badge long enough to testify."

She nodded, as if that told her what she wanted to know about him. A few moments later, they rode into a clearing that overlooked the same stream which ran past the J Bar.

Kyle pulled up.

She reined in her horse as well and looked back at him.

"You'll be going straight on down from here," Kyle told her. "Me, I'll be cutting south, back off those mountains. The way I came."

"I'll . . . see to those graves for you," she said. "And I won't forget them. I promise you."

"I'd sure appreciate that, Miss Beecher."

"I hope you'll come back someday — to your ranch. It has fine potential."

"Yes, ma'am. I reckon it has. And I

just might do that. Someday."

She nodded to him. He touched the brim of his hat and held his horse quiet as he watched her turn her horse about and continue on down the trail. After a while, just before she rode out of sight behind a stand of pine, she turned in her saddle and waved.

The publishers hope that this Large Print Book has brought you pleasurable reading. Each title is designed to make the text as easy to see as possible. G. K. Hall Large Print Books are available from your library or local bookstore or through the Large Print Book Club. If you would like a complete list of the Large Print Books we have published or information about our Book Club, please write directly to:

G. K. Hall & Co.
70 Lincoln Street
Boston, Mass. 02111